ALWAYS THE WALLFLOWER

Never the Bride
Book 5

Emily E K Murdoch

ARE YOU SIGNED UP FOR DRAGONBLADE'S BLOG?

You'll get the latest news and information on exclusive giveaways, exclusive excerpts, coming releases, sales, free books, cover reveals and more.

Check out our complete list of authors, too!

No spam, no junk. That's a promise!

Sign Up Here

www.dragonbladepublishing.com

Dearest Reader;

Thank you for your support of a small press. At Dragonblade Publishing, we strive to bring you the highest quality Historical Romance from the some of the best authors in the business. Without your support, there is no 'us', so we sincerely hope you adore these stories and find some new favorite authors along the way.

Happy Reading!

CEO, Dragonblade Publishing

Additional Dragonblade books by Author Emily E K Murdoch

Never The Bride Series
Always the Bridesmaid (Book 1)
Always the Chaperone (Book 2)
Always the Courtesan (Book 3)
Always the Best Friend (Book 4)
Always the Wallflower (Book 5)
Always the Bluestocking (Book 6)

CHAPTER ONE

THERE WAS NOTHING more Lady Letitia Cavendish could do to make herself less noticeable, and yet she shrank back as a gentleman with a ridiculous cravat walked by.

"—and Prinny said no one else had better, and of course, I agreed with him, for I had never seen..."

Letitia swallowed down the bile that had risen at the mere possibility of a gentleman speaking to her. *Shyness: what a curse.*

Her clasped hands shook, and her gray eyes looked around the room at the dancing couples. The entire day had been a dream. Harry and Monty's wedding. Lady Harriet, Duchess of Devonshire, as she should be known now. A smile crept over Letitia's face at the very thought. The two girls had grown up together, and to see her now, utterly captivated by the love of her best friend, was satisfying.

It was what Letitia had dreamed of all her life.

Something drew her attention—a gentleman. He was standing on the other side of the room, watching couples dance.

Letitia hated herself for feeling embarrassment from a mere look. A war was being waged within her, desperate to both be noticed and not noticed. *The unending, internal dispute of a wallflower.*

The gentleman was not unattractive, Letitia mused in the privacy of her own mind, *and not utterly repugnant.* He had a charming smile, which broadened as he waved.

Her cheeks heated as her shoulders hit the wall behind her. She received such little attention, after all. It would be a shame to waste it.

The man left his position at the opposing wall and started moving toward her.

Letitia's heart thundered, and she took a step forward. *Was this the moment?* The opportunity, finally, to be asked to dance by a gentleman and not to stand alone by the side?

He was nearer, and Letitia scrambled to think what to say. *Good afternoon, sir? Did you enjoy the church service, sir? Yes, what a happy couple.*

All the pleasant nothings one said at weddings. All seemed crass and inconsequential, but as she opened her mouth, hoping that the least embarrassing one would find its way to her lips, the gentleman's gaze slipped past to a young lady behind her.

"My dear Miss Eagerton, I had no idea you were in town!"

Letitia retreated to her safe position by the wall and hoped, as her cheeks burned, that no one had noticed her error. Of course, he had not stepped across the room to greet her. That simply did not happen to wallflowers like her.

The first time she had been called a wallflower had been so long ago, it was impossible to untangle the thought of it from her own self. Letitia, the wallflower. The person no one noticed. The woman who faded into the background.

This time, she spotted a gentleman who was definitely staring at her. Wasn't he? She looked around as inconspicuously as she could. There did not appear to be another lady he could be watching nearby.

Heat rose from her toes to her neck, and Letitia had a vision of her skin turning crimson. He was handsome. Perhaps he would ask her to dance—she had been standing here, after all, for the last three dances.

Perhaps he was the one, finally, who would see her for what she was. Not just a wallflower, but a young lady.

The gentleman was not alone. Beside him stood another man, less handsome but dressed in the latest fashions, and he leaned to whisper something.

They laughed, their gazes flickering to her as their humor increased.

She flushed. It was bad enough that she, bridesmaid to the new Duchess of Devonshire, was forced to remain at this wedding reception far longer than she would wish, but to be openly mocked by these rapscallions!

If only she had the talent, as so many of her friends did, of speaking her mind. There was much she could have hurled at the pair of gentlemen openly mocking her, but even considering it made her nauseous.

But she was a Cavendish, and that meant something. Letitia did not allow her head to lower as she so desperately wanted. She might always be the wallflower and never the bride, but she would not reveal her pain.

Rapid movement visible through the open door to the hallway caught her eye. There was Harry, the Duchess of Devonshire, darting with Monty behind her, and Letitia caught a scrap of their conversation.

"Well, where is she?"

"You know little Letitia, she craves inattention, not adoration. We will find her."

"She could be anywhere!"

Letitia wondered whether it was possible to cross the dance floor and sit down out of their notice, but it was too late.

"There you are!" Harry beamed as she entered the room with her husband behind her. "Letitia, thank you."

Letitia swallowed. "What for?"

"The mere reason you do not know why you are to be thanked is reason enough," Harry smiled. "But beyond that—"

"There you are!" Monty had finally disentangled himself from well-wishers and was grinning as broadly as his bride. "You found her. Thank you, Letitia."

Letitia looked from one to the other. "I-I still do not understand—"

"You are my bridesmaid," Harry reminded her.

"All I did was walk behind you, Harry."

She saw Harry and Monty exchange a pitying look, and a spark of anger rose. She did not want their pity, however well-intended. Yes, she was shy, but that did not mean she had to endure their public display of sympathy.

"They are making a set in the dining room," said Monty gently. "With the doors to this room open, it will make for at least eight couples. Can I encourage you to join them, Letitia?"

Her heart sank. She had known it would come to this—what was a party if no one was dancing? But it was her own personal hell, and Harry's warning glance was too late to prevent her husband from speaking.

Taking a deep breath, Letitia managed, "N-No one has asked me, Monty."

"Why don't you," Harry began.

"Give me a moment," said Monty, glancing around the room, "and I can—"

"Please." From somewhere within her soul, Letitia found the courage to speak, and the defiance in her tone surprised even her. Monty turned back to stare at her. "Please, Monty. I beg you. No partners out of pity."

Letitia tried to keep eye contact with her cousin, but her gaze dropped. Being a wallflower was not just uncomfortable for her; she knew it was an embarrassment to her friends and family even more so. That a Cavendish should be so plain! That a Cavendish, that noble family, was not even pretty enough to tempt a young man to dance with her for twenty minutes?

Harry was watching her with genuine concern. "Letitia—"

"Lady Harriet!"

Harry groaned, and Letitia looked up to see Mrs. Bryant, gossip of London, trying to force her way through the crowd.

"I had better go," said Monty hurriedly. "I think I am needed by—"

Letitia crept away from the confrontation, anything to escape the direct firing line of Mrs. Bryant. Thankfully, there was enough hubbub in the room to move without censure.

"You know, you will never find a gentleman to marry you like that."

Letitia jumped. Miss Mariah Wynn was seated in a nook behind her, spectacles on her nose and a book in her hands.

Letitia smiled, tension leaving her shoulders. "Hello, Mariah."

Mariah rose from her seat, put her spectacles and book in the reticle dangling from her arm, and sniffed. "No young gentlemen queuing up to dance with you, I see?"

Letitia's stomach twisted. Mariah was a good friend to her, and they had found much solace together through a shared passion for books and quiet. However, Mariah did inadvertently vex her at least five times every conversation.

"No," she said quietly. "N-No gentlemen, queuing or otherwise."

"Well, I do not suppose any of them will consider asking you, not when you look so ashamed just to be here. You are a Cavendish, for goodness sake—a *true* Cavendish."

Letitia heard the bitterness in her friend's voice but did not question it. It was known that Mariah had been adopted, but she had indicated on numerous occasions that she would not speak of her family. Letitia was not the kind of person to press such a topic.

She tried to smile. "Being a wallflower is not

so bad, I assure you. I can spend my time watching the dancing, appreciating the cleverness of movement, the—"

"Do not give me that," Mariah cut in firmly. "If you are never brave enough to speak to a gentleman you have not been introduced to, Letitia, then you are going to end up like me."

Letitia glanced at her companion. Mariah was not much older than her, perhaps by a year, although she looked older thanks to eschewing all sense of fashion.

"Like you?"

Mariah nodded. "Old maid material. Now, I have no concerns on that score, no interest in the matter. But you, Letitia, *you* want a husband, and you will never get one if you do not look a gentleman in the eyes."

It was difficult not to feel hurt at her friend's words, and Letitia reminded herself that Mariah did not speak to offend. But still…

"I do not wish to be berated," Letitia murmured, hoping no one else could hear their conversation. A pair of young ladies to their left seemed far more interested in them than necessary.

"It's not berating if it's true," Mariah said with a wry smile, "and you know I do not speak to hurt you. When I last saw a gentleman I wished to speak to, I just did. Sometimes you have to ignore your impulses."

Letitia sighed. If only she could be as brave as Mariah Wynn, a woman who never allowed society's view of her inferiority to stop her from anything.

Mariah knew her own mind and was not afraid to speak it. Letitia never did, and even when she had an opinion, it felt impossible to share.

Who wanted to hear the opinions of a young lady, even a Cavendish?

Mariah sighed heavily, and Letitia looked up to see a trio of young gentlemen, evidently a little worse for drink, stumble out of one room and into another with fits of raucous laughter.

"Men," Mariah said calmly. "Allowing them to frighten you suggests to them that they are superior. An utterly mistaken impression, and we should not permit them to form it. Your mother would tell you the same thing."

Letitia smiled. The word 'bluestocking' had been made for Mariah, and she wore it like a badge of honor. In her eyes, women could do anything.

And she was right. Her mother would tell her the same thing; it was a mercy that Lady Cavendish had not spotted her across the dance floor and loudly instructed her daughter on the best way to attract the eye of an eligible gentleman.

"It is not that I am afraid of men," Letitia

murmured, "more of the possibility they may actually wish to speak with me."

Her words sounded ridiculous even as she said them.

Mariah snorted. "All men are the same, and they are so predictable."

"Predictable?" Letitia could not conceive of a single predictable trait of the gentlemen in her acquaintance.

"They want to find a wife who is pretty, subservient, and does not think for herself," her friend sniffed. "Anyone else is just decoration or a nuisance."

A smile crept over Letitia's face. How very like Mariah. Ever since they had shared a governess when small, she had wanted to know more, learn more, and the fact that she was a young lady and not a young gentleman had not stopped her.

If only she could be more like Mariah, sure and certain—or more like Harry, vibrant and confident. Letitia twisted her fingers together. *Anything other than who she was.*

"Champagne?"

Letitia jumped. She had not noticed him approach, and the handsome footman proffered a silver platter with flutes of champagne.

"Y-Yes," she stammered, hating herself. *A servant, too? Was she to be overwhelmed by any man who spoke to her?*

Taking the glass, Letitia tried to watch the dancers in their careful steps.

There was Lady Charlotte, the Duchess of Mercia now, of course. To think that a year ago, she had been society's chaperone, never expected to wed—and there she was, dancing hand in hand with her husband, their son held by a nursemaid.

Pain twisted Letitia's heart: jealousy, an ugly emotion she could never bear to admit. Why was it so impossible to find a happily ever after?

She had seen four young ladies in her acquaintance, one of them, her dear friend Harry, marry recently, and no gentleman had even looked at her twice, other than to laugh.

Heat blossomed in her body despite the chill of the glass in her hand.

"Have you read it?"

"What?" Letitia looked wildly at her friend.

Mariah sighed. "You have not been listening to a word I have been saying, have you?" Without waiting for Letitia to reply, she continued, "I was speaking of the most exciting book that has just been published. I have borrowed it from the lending library. *A New Mathematical and Philosophical Dictionary*—does it not sound riveting?"

Letitia shook her head. "Not really, Mariah, you know my interest in mathematics is but fleeting."

"Oh, Letitia, you absolutely must dive into

this text," Mariah said, enthusiasm rushing through her words, eyes widening. "I had not been aware of some of the complexities of the formulae—to think, Letitia, almost anything can be made and unmade through the power of numbers. I had not even realized that—you are not listening to me."

"Mariah, you know I have no intellect for such things! My mind is simply not made that way, and you cannot scold me into it."

Mariah smiled. "Everyone's mind can be made to think that way. Even a woman may master the sciences, although that may surprise many I have spoken to at…"

Letitia allowed Mariah's words to wash over her. She had seen something far more intriguing on the other side of the room.

Or rather, someone. It was Edward, Viscount Wynn.

Her heart fluttered. The eligible bachelor had arrived in town but three weeks ago, and everywhere he went, there was scandal and intrigue. It did not hurt that he was remarkably handsome, but there was something more.

Letitia stared, drinking him in during this rare occasion to watch and be unseen. He was tall, far taller than her own father, with hair so dark it was almost black. His attitude was regal, the way his gaze swept across the room.

Swallowing, she tried to look away, but it

was impossible. She had developed a fascination with him as soon as he had arrived in town—a gentleman so charming and yet so disregarded by so many in society.

"Is that…"

Mariah paused and turned to look in the direction Letitia was staring, and sighed.

"Yes, that is my brother," she said heavily. "Adopted brother, of course. Viscount Wynn. 'Tis a good thing he has not spotted us, Letitia, we will not be forced to speak with him."

There was something about him, an air of complete self-importance. *That* was a gentleman who never wondered whether he was welcome in a room.

Letitia swallowed. There was a man who would sweep a young lady off their feet, and no mistake—it was a shame it would never be her. A rake would never consider a wallflower.

Mariah snorted, and Letitia jumped at the sudden sound, making her friend laugh.

"Who does he think he is," Mariah was saying, shaking her head. "He was not invited to this wedding, and I know that for a fact. I asked Lady Harriet when I saw her last week at Almack's, and I did not see him in the church. I should go over and tell him he is not welcome. Will you join me, Letitia?"

Panic rose in her heart. "No, leave him be. I am sure Harry would not mind an extra guest, and there is plenty of food for everyone. Viscount Wynn is—"

But her voice broke off. As she had spoken his name, the viscount had turned, and his gaze met hers.

Letitia gasped. It was a visceral reaction, as though he was beside her and had touched her arm. How was it possible to have such a strong response to a gentleman from a look alone? But his dark brown eyes were locked on hers, and Letitia could not look away.

He smiled. Muttering something to the young lady beside him, he started making his way around the room toward them.

Letitia could barely breathe. *Was this the moment she would remember forever, the moment they would tell their children about—how their father saw their mama across a crowded dance chamber and knew from one look they were meant to be together?*

"Mariah." Viscount Wynn inclined his head at his sister, and both Mariah and Letitia curtsied.

By the time they had risen, the Viscount had gone.

Letitia's heart, fluttering only a moment ago, now seemed to have descended to her stomach. *Of course, he was not about to ask her to dance.* The mere thought was ridiculous, and she should have crushed it immediately.

What an expectation! He would undoubtedly wish to dance with beautiful young ladies, elegant ones who could flirt and laugh.

"Really, Letitia," Mariah spoke kindly for the first time in their conversation. "My adoptive brother is the biggest rake in town, always looking to break someone's heart. You should be grateful you are not in his sights, for I have heard he cares as little for reputations as for the hearts he breaks."

Letitia swallowed, attempting to regain control. This fancy she had for Viscount Wynn would always be unrequited. It was foolish, a childish obsession she must ignore. He probably did not even know who she was.

Mariah frowned as she watched him meander around the room. "Edward never welcomed me into his family when his parents adopted me, and we barely speak now. In fact, I think that is the longest conversation we have had this year. *That* is the measure of the man Viscount Wynn is."

Letitia smiled weakly as she watched the back of him disappear. "It matters not, Mariah, I would not worry yourself. To him, or any other gentleman of my acquaintance, I will always be the wallflower and never the bride."

CHAPTER TWO

I T WAS IMPOSSIBLE to prevent the yawn, and Edward, Viscount Wynn, did nothing to quell it.

God's teeth, he thought, shifting position to keep awake. He could have been anywhere, anywhere in London. He was welcome in almost every respectable home—and a smile crept over his face at the thought of the fathers who would do anything to keep him out of their drawing rooms.

There were plenty of gentleman's clubs, which were desperate to have him on their members' list. He had the missives somewhere in his desk at Redmont.

In short, he had not lacked opportunities to enjoy himself this evening, a cold one near the end of the Season, and he knew the name Wynn would open doors.

And yet, he was here. *Almack's*. Wynn shivered as the smells of the room filled his nostrils, pomanders, grease paint, cigars, and the heat of dancing bodies.

Wynn forced down the next yawn if only to save himself the disgust of breathing in such an unpleasant mixture.

Wednesday evening, and he was bored out of his skin.

A laughing group walked past, gaining his attention by containing at least three ladies of impressive beauty, but they were gone before he could consider what retort would capture their attention.

No matter. There were no new faces here.

To think he could have been at the St. Mark's Club. Someone had mentioned there was gaming on Wednesdays, one which he would have surely won.

"Anyone take your fancy?"

He had never seen a gentleman outdo him in cards. If he had attended St. Mark's Club instead of being swayed into attending Almack's—that damned voucher with Lady Romeril's handwriting spiked along the side, 'We will expect you'— he would have filled his pockets with guineas by now.

Not that he needed it. The Wynn estate had never been better, now that his father had died and stopped selling off the most precious land.

He sighed. *No, it was the chase that was the fun.*

Cards and women.

Quite the opposite of Almack's.

"I said, anyone take your fancy, Wynn?"

His dark eyes swept around the room. Almack's had not changed in years; it was like walking into a living museum. He could remember the first time his parents had brought him here. The drapes were the same, the food, even the music.

Like a fly trapped in amber. They said it was because Prinny liked it that way, but Wynn could not remember the last time the Regent had been seen here. Certainly not in the last year.

A wry smile crept over his face as he took in the far left corner, packed with gossiping women all over the age of five and thirty. *The Mamas.* There they stood, desperate to marry off their daughters and not just to the richest and most respected gentleman. An ideal suitor would also possess power.

One caught his eye, her gaze fixed on an awkward chit of a thing dancing with a much older gentleman, who was leering at his partner.

Something unsettled in his stomach. *Even better, make him old and likely to die in the next few years. There was nothing like inheriting a competency.*

Wynn's eyes drifted to the other side of the room, and he shook his head. There were the gentlemen of the *ton,* the male counterparts of the Mamas, but matrimony was not their topic of choice.

It would be power and politics. It was possible to see, if one concentrated, the line between the Whigs and the Tories. You could start to see the patterns. Who was not speaking with whom, who received a cold shoulder when they attempted to approach a group.

"Can you hear me?"

And between the two sets of parents, the dancers. Wynn almost laughed aloud at the idiots in rows, prancing up and down with the eyes of respectable society on them.

It was all a game, much like the cards he so enjoyed. How close could a gentleman get to his partner without either the lady protesting—and he had heard tell of a woman slapping a gentleman for being too eager—or her Mama sweeping her away, determined to keep her honor intact?

A game, a dance, a dare…

Wynn sighed. Matrimony or money-making, that was all life in London boiled down to.

It was difficult to remember why he had even bothered to return after staying away for two long years. Had he hoped there would be a sudden change in the way society operated?

He had been a fool if he had.

All women were the same. In his one and thirty years, he had seen nothing to suggest there was a single lady who thought differently, her mind not filled with nonsense, frippery, gowns, balls, and how to snare a husband.

Wynn watched a pair at the end, clearly uninterested in each other but standing for decorum's sake. It was so ridiculous; you could see exactly what any woman wanted from a mile off.

It inevitably boiled down to one of three things: more wealth, more power, and more children. There was only one way to secure those things, and that was matrimony.

"Wynn, are you quite well?"

His gaze wandered along the set and was caught by a woman of startling beauty. She danced with abandon, laughing at what her partner had said, attracting the attention of the gentlemen around her.

He did not blame them. He was captivated, too, even from this distance. Her eyes darted over to him, and she smiled coquettishly.

Wynn grinned. He recognized a flirt when he saw one. A tiger always knows a tiger.

Now that he looked more closely, he recognized her. It was Miss Emma Tilbury, and he saw with disappointment the rumors were undoubtedly true.

Miss Tilbury was no longer under the protection of the Earl of Marnmouth. It was enough to see the frayed edges of her gown, the diamonds around her neck sparkling a little less like diamonds and a little more like glass.

She was still beautiful, but her beauty had faded. Inevitable after being the mistress of a man for so long, cast off without a word.

But where did that leave her? She danced like her life depended on it, that smile a little too desperate for Wynn's tastes.

He looked away. He had enough women fawning over him and did not need more—a woman who evidently needed a gentleman's protection—to misunderstand his interest.

"Should I go, then?"

But he would be a liar if he said he didn't like it. Wynn smiled at a memory from last week. *What was her name, Miss Gardener? Miss Grandienne?* It did not matter, for he had enticed her into the garden of his hosts, the Howards, and spent a rather delicious twenty minutes kissing her so passionately, he was rather certain he had ruined her.

What was not to like about being a rake? All the pleasures of women without any of the responsibility.

But Almack's was the opposite, all the responsibility to be respectable with none of the fun. Every chit on her best behavior, desperate not to embarrass herself and secure a husband.

Wynn fought down another yawn. The only woman who had ever managed to break that mold was his adopted sister. Mariah Wynn did not care what anyone thought of her and was quite blatant in her disregard for him.

His bluestocking sister was the last person who would—

"What the devil's the matter with you?"

Wynn started at the fierce tone and looked at his companion. The Duke of Axwick, as tall as he was and just as dark, was staring at him as though he was possessed.

"What?"

Axwick laughed. "God's teeth, man, I have been attempting to engage you in conversation for the last five minutes, and you have been lost to the world! Any particular lady on your mind?"

Wynn joined with his laughter. "I should think not, old man—not unless any fresh young ladies have come out into society in the last week?"

"I rather think they would have had themselves introduced at St. James's at the beginning of the Season," Axwick said dryly, his gaze taking in the rabble in the room. "Not much point entering society at the end, is there?"

Wynn shook his head. "In that case, no. I am disappointed to report there are no ladies in Almack's or in London, able to tempt me."

"You are far too particular!"

"If anything, I am not particular enough," Wynn interjected with a grin. "My reputation of a dastardly rake precedes me, and I will admit, a small part of me is proud."

Axwick snorted, and Wynn's grin broadened.

"Well, perhaps more than a little proud," he admitted, stepping back with his friend as a gaggle of laughing ladies hurried past them.

"You are God's gift to women, then?"

Wynn nodded. "Well, they say that a Wynn always wins. But that does not mean I will seduce any woman up for tupping. I have some standards, though they are admittedly low."

He laughed, but Axwick frowned and kept silent. A little too late, Wynn remembered his friend had undergone a change of heart since the last time he was in town.

Two years ago, Axwick—who was in some way a distant cousin, although they could not remember how—had been dark, dismal, and content to stay at home. He had sworn off women in general and matrimony specifically, did not drink, did not gamble…

Wynn remembered them spending hours debating what to do, before realizing the entire evening had disappeared in the discussion.

And then the elder of the two admitted he had not only fallen in love but *married*.

"I spoke rashly," Wynn said quietly. "I do apologize, Axwick. You know I would never treat a true lady like that—but I have needs."

Axwick's smile was forced. "You did not speak rashly, my friend, you spoke without thinking with whom you spoke."

"Perhaps. But I won't again."

As the music stopped and the dancers were applauded, Axwick spoke again. "Come now, you have to dance. If you do not dance at Almack's, were you even here?"

Wynn groaned. "I do not wish to spend twenty minutes of my life—twenty minutes that I will never get back, mind!—listening to a girl chatter on about her gown or the busyness of the room—"

"Or the cost of her gloves," Axwick added.

"Or even worse," Wynn said with a sigh, "how eligible she is. God's teeth, man, I do not know how you bear it. You come here every week?"

It was challenging to think of anything much worse.

Axwick shrugged. "I have a reputation to maintain, Wynn, something you know little about. 'Tis fine for you to stay hidden in that pile of yours in the country, but others have to maintain our positions. Tabitha is fortunate, she has the excuse of our child to hide away from the world. I have to come here, stand, and look impressive."

"Which you do well."

The sarcastic tone was not lost on Axwick, who rolled his eyes. "Now, let us see if we can find you a partner."

"Why can't you dance?" Wynn protested. "If you are for it, why—"

"I am an old married man," countered Axwick, who was not yet six and thirty. "My dancing days are over. It would be most unseemly to offer my hand to another woman. You, on the other hand, are one of the most eligible gentlemen in town. You must have heard the gossip?"

Wynn demurred, but his ego was flattered.

"I see you have," said Axwick shrewdly. "Now, who would…ah, yes. Devonshire!"

A gentleman a few yards away turned and smiled at Axwick. After a few words of apology to his companions, he strode over.

Wynn could not help but be intrigued. Axwick was one of the highest houses with which he was acquainted—the Devonshires were a truly noble house, one of the oldest. He had never been introduced to any of its members, and if he was not mistaken, he was about to be introduced to its head.

As the gentleman bowed, Wynn examined him with a careful eye. He was handsome and relaxed as only a gentleman born to the heights of privilege could be.

"Devonshire, may I introduce my friend and third cousin once removed—"

"Or first cousin three times removed," interjected Wynn with a lazy grin. "Neither of us is sure."

"Edward, Viscount Wynn," finished Axwick with a smile. "Wynn, I have the honor of introducing Montague Cavendish, the seventeenth Duke of Devonshire."

The two gentlemen bowed again, but before Wynn could say anything, Axwick continued.

"My friend here is looking for a dance partner," said Axwick, smiling knowingly at Devonshire. "I wondered whether your cousin would be interested in being introduced."

Devonshire raised an eyebrow. "Lady Letitia Cavendish?"

A hint of interest warmed in Wynn's stomach. Lady Letitia Cavendish…he had never heard of her before, but by mere virtue of her name, she was someone worth knowing. The Cavendish family was known for beauty, wit, and wealth.

For all of his talk that there were no young ladies left to be introduced to, it certainly could not hurt to meet her, and her wit would be a pleasant distraction from the monotony of the evening.

"I would be honored to be introduced to the Lady Letitia," Wynn said aloud with a quick nod. "If she would stand with me."

Devonshire smiled. "My cousin would certainly like to dance, I am sure of it. Please excuse me, gentlemen, and I will fetch her."

Before Wynn could say another word, Devonshire had bowed and departed from their company.

Wynn whistled slowly. "God in Heaven, Axwick, I did not know you were that well connected."

Axwick laughed, lifting a drink from a platter. "If you live in London, you cannot help but know people. I tell you, Wynn, Lady Letitia is a genteel woman, and you should treat her that way."

A mischievous grin crept over Wynn's face. "My dear man, you know I cannot promise not to seduce a Cavendish, not when…"

His voice trailed away as his eyes fell upon Devonshire, returning hand in hand with a young woman who evidently did not want to be joining them.

"Monty, let me go," she muttered, her eyes wide and staring.

Wynn's heart sank. She was plain, plain even for Almack's. *God be damned, this was Lady Letitia? This unadorned chit?*

He had seen her when he had invited himself to the Devonshires' wedding reception, seen her conversing with Mariah—but he had taken her for a servant girl, her gown had been so uninteresting and her presence so uninspired. No jewelry at all, and a hunted look as though she did not belong.

He had walked straight past her, nodded at Mariah as he knew his mother would have wanted, and gone on his way.

To think that she was a Cavendish!

Devonshire smiled, his grip still firmly on Lady Letitia's hand as she struggled to retreat.

"I have the pleasure of introducing you to my cousin," he said. "Lady Letitia Cavendish."

For the first time in his life, Wynn felt awkward. Bowing his head quickly and hoping to God she would reject his hand once he made the offer to dance, by the time he looked up, her face was pink.

Oh, God, Wynn thought dully. *One of those.* Too embarrassed to say anything, too shy to contribute to the conversation—the wallflowers of society.

Trust him to be parceled off to a wallflower, but what could he do? He would have to dance with her, and just cross his fingers it would be a short one.

This was a good lesson in not accepting a lady's hand before seeing her. Not even if she was the cousin of a nobleman.

Not even if she was a Cavendish.

Plastering a stiff smile across his face, Wynn proffered his hand. "Lady Letitia, would you do the honor of standing with me for this next dance?"

For a heart-stopping moment, he actually thought she was going to refuse him. Her gray eyes jerked toward her cousin as though begging him to be relieved of this arduous duty, and a prickle of irritation rose in Wynn. *She* did not wish to dance with *him?*

"My cousin would be delighted," Devonshire said hastily, pulling Lady Letitia forward so rapidly that she was obliged to reach out a hand to steady herself—which fell into Wynn's extended one.

Wynn kept his face as calm as possible. "The honor is all mine."

Enough pleasantries. The music was starting up, and Wynn walked toward the set with her on his arm.

Well, it could not harm his reputation in the long run. She may be plain, with rather startling red hair pulled back in what could not be described as the latest fashion, but she was a Cavendish.

After placing her in the row of ladies, Wynn turned to face her and tried to smile—but she did not return the compliment. In fact, unlike every other young lady with whom he had ever danced, she did not smile, blush at his attentions, or try to impress him with a witticism.

Lady Letitia Cavendish stood there, silent, her eyes on the ground. As the music started and they bowed and curtsied to each other, he expected her to simper, but no. The most meager curtsey without even catching his eye.

"Are you enjoying the evening?" he asked.

This was her moment to shine if she wanted to—but instead of melting in his gaze and giggling at the attention, she nodded.

In all other respects, she gave no sign she had heard him. She could have been standing up with anyone.

With anyone. The thought burned in Wynn's mind. How dare she—he was Viscount Wynn! He could see a few ladies who were watching him with great interest, and his irritation piqued.

"Your gown is elegant," he said stiffly as they joined hands to walk in a circle.

Lady Letitia did not raise her head. "Thank you."

She was the most prickly thing he had ever met, and Wynn could not deny her evident disinterest in him was intriguing.

Women loved him; they always had, and he had never struggled to entertain. He may be bored of them, bored of hearing the same simpering fawning words, but that did not mean he did not want to hear them.

But not Lady Letitia. She evidently wished to draw no attention to herself, and Wynn could not help but be fascinated.

As they paraded down the set, he looked at her more closely and made a startling discovery.

Lady Letitia Cavendish was not plain.

It was easy to think that if one just took a glance. Everything about her dress and toilette seemed designed to avoid attention, to be dull and pale, to fall into the background.

When one looked beyond that, she was quite startling. Her gray eyes were bright, intelligent. Her lips were soft, pink, and virginal. Something in Wynn's stomach stirred as their hands parted, and she clasped hands with the gentleman to his left.

"Lady Letitia, I think you know my sister," he said quietly as they came together again, this time in an earnest attempt to draw her into conversation.

But she was not so easily fooled. "Adopted sister," she said quietly.

This was unheard of. Wynn had never failed to entertain a young lady before, never failed to make her laugh, bring a flush to her cheeks, or make her invite him to kiss her.

Lady Letitia looked more likely to fall asleep in his presence.

"Is there no topic I can draw you to speak on?" His voice was harsher than he meant, but really. This was ridiculous.

She did not seem to care. "I am not a conversationalist."

"Well, I should have expected nothing better," he said finally, snapping with irritation, "from a wallflower."

She stopped dead in the dance, the lady to her left quickly darting around her to prevent a collision.

Lady Letitia glared, her eyes fierce.

Wynn took a step back. No one had ever glared at him like that.

After a lifetime of easily charming women, he was now faced with one who simply would not be charmed.

"I—I apologize, Lady Letitia," he said awkwardly, moving toward her to keep his voice low. "I should not have said… I am sorry."

She stared as though he was a piece of dirt she had found on her shoe.

She was a firebrand, one who had never sparked before, but there was true passion there, hidden under the desire to be unseen.

Lady Letitia Cavendish was a woman he had never expected.

"Lady Letitia," he began.

Without saying a word, she turned on her heels and strode away.

"Lady Letitia!" Wynn shouted, desperate to stop her, to explain.

After a brief word with Devonshire, whose eyes quickly snapped over to him, Lady Letitia walked out of Almack's.

An uncomfortable heat rose up the back of Wynn's neck as he attempted to smile, moving out of the dance set as he no longer had a partner.

Murmurs surrounded him as onlookers attempted to guess what he could have possibly said to warrant such a reaction, but Wynn did not care.

His thoughts were on Lady Letitia. No one had ever wanted to walk away from him before.

Perhaps Lady Letitia was no wallflower after all.

CHAPTER THREE

"I T WAS QUITE a dull affair."

Even to Letitia's ears, her words were not convincing—and Harry raised an eyebrow.

"A dull affair? Almack's, near the end of the Season, with every young thing desperate to prove their worth?" Harry sniffed. "It does not sound likely, Letitia. What happened?"

It was all she could do to prevent weariness from seeping into her words, but then she had been fielding questions for almost an hour.

"Nothing happened," she said more firmly.

Lady Harriet was not accustomed to being told no, and certainly not from Letitia. Their friendship went back to the cradle, and that meant—to Letitia's disappointment—she was not so easily fooled.

"I cannot believe it," she said with a smile. "Something always happens at Almack's!"

Letitia's gaze drifted away, unwilling to make

eye contact while attempting to lie. Harry snorted and dropped her own gaze to the embroidery in her hands, picking up her needle and stabbing it forcefully through one section with a look of irritation.

"You know I will just keep on asking."

Letitia sighed. She needed to change the conversation now. "If you were so interested in what could happen at Almack's last night, it would have been well for you to attend yourself. What are you working on? It looks elegant."

It was one of the longest speeches Letitia had ever made under such duress, but Harry merely kept working.

"Hateful thing, is it not?" she said cheerfully. "I never enjoyed needlework as a child, and I hate it even more as an adult."

"Then why do it?"

Harry shrugged. "'Tis less dull than many other things. I was not feeling well last night, Letitia, as well you know, and so it was not possible to attend. Most irritating. Monty told me he met Viscount Wynn—you know, the rake who has finally returned to town?"

Throat dry, Letitia's gaze dropped to her hands, twisted uselessly in her lap. Just hearing his name was enough to take her right back to that moment. She had stood up with Viscount Wynn, had her chance to impress him, and what had she done?

Stalked away like a petulant child.

"Did you meet him or any other gentlemen of interest?"

Letitia swallowed. She had been a fool to come here, but Harry's invitation had been so insistent. And she was family now. One could not decline an invitation from family.

"N-No one of note," she managed before her voice failed her, and she reached along the sofa to pick up another piece of embroidery. "Is…is this your own work?"

"What?" Harry glanced up at it and grinned. "Lord, no, that is one of Lady Honora's pieces— you know, the Countess of Chester?"

"Is it really? It is beautiful," said Letitia gratefully. "I do admire the way she—"

"And you did not meet Viscount Wynn?"

Her damned body—Letitia had always hated the lack of control she had of her own flesh. *Why, oh, why did it have to pink? Why did it so easily give her away?*

More importantly, why had other people learned how to lie, and lie easily, and yet she had never developed a talent for it?

"No," she managed.

Harry sighed heavily. The duchess's eyes were darting between the embroidery in her hands and the pattern on a crumpled piece of paper to her left.

"It does not seem possible that you did not

run into *anyone*," she said. "Who did you speak to?"

If only she could move the conversation to something else—anything else! Letitia's pulse throbbed in her ears, her breathing shallow. She had no wish to lie, but how else would she avoid these direct questions?

She could not reveal the truth, but how much longer would she have to suffer through this interrogation?

"It was...it was a quiet affair," Letitia managed with a smile. "Honestly, Harry, you know what Almack's is like near the end of the Season. 'Tis...'tis far more likely that people are attending private balls than public ones."

She swallowed. With every response concealing what had really happened between her and Viscount Wynn, the more her mind drifted toward him.

Just the thought of him made prickles of heat flutter all over her body. He had been so tall, so domineering, and his words had caused her such pain.

She would not have believed it possible to embarrass herself so thoroughly in ten minutes, but of course, she had managed it.

Letitia could not remember the last time she had danced in public—it must have been almost three years ago. No wonder she had made a fool of herself; embarrassment was an unavoidable result of her standing up.

If only it had been because of her charming words that she felt such a rush, or perhaps because she had danced a few steps out of time that she had been embarrassed.

Why had she abandoned Viscount Wynn in the middle of the set at Almack's, completely alone, because he had offended her?

"Almack's? Quiet affair?"

Harry's words hardly registered as Letitia descended into a silent panic of remembrance. And what was it that Viscount Wynn had done to offend her?

He had talked to her!

Worse, he had attempted to flatter her. If he had known her, he would not have bothered.

It was clear he had not seen her as a potential seduction, certainly not a woman he could court and bed, as he had done to so many other young ladies of the *ton* if the rumors were true.

Not that Letitia would have allowed him to do such a thing.

Without warning, without conscious thought, her mind was suddenly filled with wild thoughts of how Viscount Wynn could seduce her. *His hands, moving across her, his mouth whispering desperately delicious things, his lips lowering down to hers...*

"I know you, Letitia."

She jumped. Harry was staring with a shrewd

smile.

"M-Me?" Letitia managed.

Harry nodded. "Do not think you can hide it from me, girl, we have known each other more than twenty years! You have met a gentleman, have you not?"

Her heart thundered in her chest. "Of course not."

But the duchess smiled as she laid down her needlework. "I do not know why you deny it, Letitia, 'tis hardly a crime nor a sin. What is his name?"

Letitia swallowed. "No one."

Her treacherous mind returned once more to Viscount Wynn. He was such a figure of a gentleman, she had never seen anyone like him, and she had been given one chance—just one!— to impress him.

"I have the pleasure of introducing you to my cousin, Lady Letitia Cavendish."

Heat flashed through her like a wave as the memory of that stilted introduction by her cousin came back to her. It was too cruel of Monty to force her into that position. He knew how discomforted she felt in the presence of strangers.

If she had kept her head, she could have been kissed last night by Viscount Wynn...

Letitia blinked. She had lost all concentration, and Harry was smiling in a dreadfully knowing way. It was unfair that Harry should know her *that* well.

Determined to take her companion's attention away from her for just one minute, Letitia cast about desperately in her mind for another topic—and found one.

"Have you heard that the lending library on Piccadilly has received a new delivery?"

Harry's eyes brightened. "Are you sure? I did not believe they were due to receive anything until Saturday."

Letitia nodded eagerly. "I-I heard it from Lady Romeril, and you know she is always most precise about such things. I wonder whether they have received any novels."

"Or scientific works for your friend, Miss Wynn."

A small smile crept over Letitia's face. Mariah was quite unique in that respect.

She said instead, "Why not go down to Piccadilly and visit the lending library? It would be a shame to miss the latest additions because we were not circumspect enough to visit in time."

Letitia saw the mingled desire and hesitation in Harry's face.

"I had not anticipated a long walk today," Harry said with a glance at the window. Sunlight was streaming through it. "Although I will admit, the weather is fine."

"'Tis only a short walk," she said quickly, relieved to have found a topic that adequately distracted her friend from gentlemen and balls. "I insist, Harry—and we can call for the carriage for the return trip if we feel fatigued."

Harry considered the proposal.

"Well," she said bracingly, "'tis better than embroidery. Ring the bell, Letitia, and we will venture out!"

There were unending conversations before they left—agreeing with the cook exactly what was to be served for dinner, informing the butler of their intended destination, and declaring to the coachman that he may be required to meet them at Piccadilly in just over an hour's time.

It was a wonder, Letitia thought as they finally left, *Harry managed to go anywhere.* But there was a small part of her, one she would never admit, which envied this majestic rule over her own domain.

At home, Letitia had to beg permission to ask a servant a thing, even if it was her own lady's maid. Her father was still the king in his own land.

"There we are," said Harry, interrupting Letitia's thoughts as they turned a corner. "I was so thrilled when the lending library opened here. There is one in Bath, of course, and one further across town, but I much prefer having one here, a few streets away. Do you think they will have another copy of *Hebrew Melodies*, by Lord Byron?"

"I do hope so," said Letitia warmly as they

made their way toward its impressive doors. "It is a sanctuary, a lending library, and there is never enough Byron to go around."

A sigh of relief escaped her lips when they stepped over the threshold and into the silence of the place. In all her visits with Mariah, Letitia had never seen a gentleman. Here at least, she would be safe.

Why would men bother? They purchased their books; they did not borrow them.

Letitia saw a few familiar faces and felt the tension in her shoulders disappear. The lending library was a rare refuge from the gazes of men, which she was met with everywhere else she went.

No dancing, no forced conversation, no opportunity to be a wallflower. Just herself and books.

"Well met, Lady Letitia."

She twisted around in horror to see the owner of that voice—a voice she knew, though she had heard it but once before.

Viscount Wynn was standing behind her, leaning against a shelf with a book in his hand and a smile on his face. He was even more handsome than she had remembered, and in the daylight streaming through the window, his almost-black hair shone.

"I-I did not...I did not see you..." She hated her voice for being so insipid. *Why was it impossible to speak when confronted with a gentleman outside her small and intimate acquaintance?*

And Viscount Wynn, of all people?

He smiled and took a step toward her. "Oh, dear, Lady Letitia. Cat got your tongue?"

"Letitia? Oh, there you are! Yes, they have another copy of—oh." Harry's voice trailed away as she saw an unknown gentleman staring at her companion. "Letitia, will you not introduce us?"

Letitia swallowed. It was all too much—she had come here precisely to avoid conversation *about* Viscount Wynn, and now here she was, literally faced with him!

"H-Harry," Letitia said weakly, attempting to communicate with a terrified look that she needed to be rescued from the situation.

"Your Grace, allow me the honor of introducing myself," Viscount Wynn's voice spoke smoothly behind Letitia. "Your husband was so good as to introduce me to his cousin, Lady Letitia, last night at Almack's. I am Edward, Viscount Wynn, and I am your servant."

He bowed, which Harry returned with an elegant curtsey. These pleasantries over, Letitia stared between them as they silently looked at her.

The wild desire to run away and leave them both flashed through her mind. She had stepped into one of her nightmares!

The attempt to avoid questions about him

had led her right to him.

"It is a pleasure to make your acquaintance," Harry said in the silence. "And are you here for a specific book, Viscount Wynn, or perusing to see the latest delivery?"

"Neither," he replied with a smile at Letitia. "Far more selfishly, I am here to see who I may meet."

Letitia's cheeks burned, and she wished for the courage to step outside and go home—but social decorum dictated, now that they were in a conversation, that it was not so easily abandoned.

"Well, I am in hunt of Lord Byron," said Harry with a laugh. "His poetry, that is, rather than his person. I will leave you to converse with Lady Letitia, Viscount Wynn. And if the two of you decide to take a walk together, I can find my own way home."

Before Letitia could say anything, the duchess had wandered down a different aisle.

She could feel Viscount Wynn's gaze on the back of her neck.

This was intolerable. She could not possibly stand in public and have a conversation with him. He was too knowing, too teasing, too attractive.

As though unable to resist, she turned to face him. There was a broad smile on his face, but it was not unkind.

"What a pleasure to meet you here, Lady Letitia," he said in a low voice. "Just the person I had wished to see."

She would not allow herself to be mocked, not by this ingrate who had offended her the night before.

"I am sure you were just as eager to see me."

"No," Letitia said. She hardly knew the word was going to escape her lips, but she had thought it so determinedly that her mouth obeyed.

She saw the look of surprise in his face as he moved closer to her. Letitia took a step back and found a bookshelf impeding her way.

"Is there an author whom you greatly en-joy?" he asked, his dark brown eyes not wavering from hers. "Lord Byron, perhaps, like your friend, the Duchess of Devonshire?"

She swallowed. He was charming, and there was no point in denying it. His presence alone was enough to make her knees feel weak, and that smile…it made her want to rush toward him.

The attraction was so deep she could almost see it. She wanted to be closer to him, to hear him speak, to laugh at his jokes.

Was this what prey felt like while entrapped in the gaze of its predator?

"No one in particular," she managed. Her words sounded hollow, almost bored, and she saw with a flicker of delight that Viscount Wynn looked a little affronted.

"No one in particular," he repeated softly. "Well then, what book have you read most recently?"

Letitia's heart was starting to flutter. *Why was he paying attention to her?* She was not pretty, nor charming, nor desirous of his attentions. She was not one of the célèbres of town, nor was she an exciting conversationalist like Miss Emma Tilbury, nor a great beauty like the Duchess of Mercia.

What did he want?

She swallowed. "*A New Mathematical and Philosophical Dictionary.* And you?"

Viscount Wynn smiled. "I cannot make you out, Lady Letitia. And I want to."

"I am sorry to disappoint you, sir," she said coldly. "Good day."

She had bobbed a brief curtsey and stepped out of the lending library before Viscount Wynn had realized what was happening, but Letitia was not so fortunate to lose his attention.

If anything, she had piqued it. Before she had taken ten steps along the pavement, a voice sounded at her side.

"Lady Letitia, you walked away from me. Why?"

Viscount Wynn's long legs had the advantage of her. She knew no matter how fast she attempted to escape him, he would always keep up.

"I have no interest in being the object of your pity, Viscount Wynn, and I will thank you for leaving me alone."

"Leave you alone? When I am escorting you home?"

His words had barely finished when Letitia gasped. He had taken her hand and placed it on her arm.

She stopped dead, staring. He had a serious look on his face.

"You know, you are most intriguing, Lady Letitia," he murmured.

Letitia tried to swallow, but her mouth was dry. People were rushing by, impossibly fast, as though time had slowed.

"I am not," she managed to gasp.

Viscount Wynn smiled without mockery. "You know, I have never been more interested in a young lady before this moment—and I am serious. You know what they say, I always Wynn."

Letitia pulled her arm away half-heartedly, but the viscount had a firm grip. His strength was overwhelming.

Viscount Wynn leaned a little closer, and she breathed him in. "I am going to court you, Lady Letitia."

His words did not make sense.

"No, you—you must not do that," she whispered, her eyes unable to leave his own.

"Why not?" he countered. "Do you not want me to?"

She had never felt like this before, for a tingling heat spread throughout her body, and she wanted nothing more than to lean closer and breathe him in again—perhaps so close that their lips would touch.

His lips turned upward in a smile. Was this all a game to him? Was this a way of passing the time when bored in a lending library, choosing a helpless girl to flirt with?

"Lady Letitia, I do believe you are frightened of me."

Viscount Wynn's words were almost a whisper, more breathed than spoken.

Letitia could not help it. She nodded.

His other hand covered hers on his arm. "I will make it my mission to make you comfortable around me."

"Y-You must not," she managed to blurt. "Why…why would you want to do that?"

He smiled. "Because I am going to pursue you, Letitia, and it is far more convenient for both of us if you are not terrified of the sight of me."

Letitia stared, fascinated. *Was he in earnest? Why on earth would he be? What could he gain by wishing to court her?*

"Come now," Viscount Wynn said smartly in a louder voice, breaking the spell between them and making Letitia jump. "You should be at home, Lady Letitia, 'tis almost luncheon, and your parents will undoubtedly be wondering where you are."

Her arm still in his, he started walking, and she had no choice but to walk with him. She did, however, manage to find her voice.

"I am having luncheon with the Devonshires," she said timidly.

Viscount Wynn smiled and took the next left. "A charming couple. I do hope to get to know them better, as I spend more time with you."

Was he truly going to attempt to court her?

Words utterly failed her. It was impossible to speak to such a man. He was everything she wanted in a husband, but she was too accustomed to being a wallflower than a young lady with whom a gentleman actually wanted to converse.

"Here we are."

Letitia blinked. Somehow, they had arrived at Cavendish Square.

"And now," Viscount Wynn said quietly, "I would like you to thank me for accompanying you all this way."

She looked up and saw a sparkle of laughter in his eyes. Something emboldened her, something she did not understand.

"I do not see why," she said, feeling nowhere near as calm as she sounded. "You have merely walked with me. If anything, you should be thanking me."

The viscount dropped her arm. "Why, there is more to you than I originally—"

"There you are!"

Both Viscount Wynn and Letitia turned to see Harry at the open front door.

"I took the carriage when I realized you had both left without me," said Harry, "and thought you would not take too long. Thank you for accompanying my friend, Viscount Wynn."

"The pleasure was truly all mine."

He bowed, and Letitia could not help but stare. What did he want—and what did she want from him?

"Nevertheless," Harry smiled, "I must make amends. Join us for dinner. Sunday, seven o'clock."

This was all too ridiculous. First a forced introduction at Almack's, now an unwelcome walk home together, next, a dinner with her most intimate friends?

Was Viscount Wynn going to be everywhere she went?

She turned to him, hoping he could sense her discomfort and do the gentlemanly thing and decline.

His dark brown eyes darted to her, and there was that smile again. "My dear Lady Harriet, I accept."

CHAPTER FOUR

WYNN'S MOUTH FELL open in an undignified manner as a trail of footmen swept into the dining room, holding the sixth course of the evening.

Groaning under his breath, he wondered whether it would be uncivilized to undo a few waistcoat buttons. A glance up and down the table told him no one else had stooped so low, and he sighed heavily.

He was unaccustomed to such finery, such levels of gluttony. It was usually bread and cheese for him, along with whatever meat his cook could find.

Not at the table of the Duke of Devonshire, of course.

Wynn smiled weakly. When the Duchess of Devonshire had invited him to dine three days ago, he had eagerly accepted. *What fool would not want a seat at the Devonshire's table?*

He had pictured Letitia and himself seated around a quiet table as conversation flowed.

A chance to finally put his ridiculous obsession with her to rest.

A chance to get to know her, see her in her natural and awkward setting, and attempt to understand why she captured his interest in such an intoxicating way.

And then move on. That had been his intention.

But he could not have imagined the countless faces which he did not recognize, or Lady Letitia in conversation with an older gentleman, who looked like he could have been her grandfather.

Now they were seated around the huge dining table, over twenty of them, and while Wynn attempted to eat through the numerous and never-ending courses, he had not managed a single word of conversation with Letitia.

Wynn wondered whether it was fate that had kept him seated so far from Letitia or his hostess.

"Are you not going to eat that?"

Wynn started. The gentleman opposite him was staring at his plate—covered, now he looked at it, with a strange sort of dumpling he did not recognize and a smear of meat—with unbridled covetousness.

Wynn smiled weakly. "Please, sir, help yourself."

The gentleman leaned forward. Wynn attempted not to smile. London truly was different from the country. Everyone had told him so, even Mariah, and he rarely listened to her on any subject. Even Axwick had warned him, and he had ignored him.

"Oh, Letitia, you jest, surely!"

Wynn's stomach contracted as his gaze went unwillingly to Letitia. She sat at the right-hand side of the Duchess of Devonshire—a woman he simply could not call 'Harry,' despite her request—looking utterly radiant.

Her fiery red hair was pinned back with an assortment of diamonds, and her gown, plain and simple, suited her perfectly. It sought neither to flatter nor to hide. It was functionality itself, and Wynn had never seen a young lady so perfectly dressed.

She laughed, and his stomach contracted painfully.

Damnit, was he so weak? He had wooed, courted, and bedded more women than there were people around this dinner table, and yet Lady Letitia Cavendish—the wallflower of the *ton*—was catching his eye in a way he could not explain.

This chit of a girl he did not even know a fortnight ago. *How did she have such a hold on him?*

"Perhaps you will enjoy the fish course more," said a dry voice.

Tabitha St. Maur, the Duchess of Axwick,

smiled. "Do not worry. You are not the first to be a little overwhelmed by Monty's eagerness to feed."

"I-I…" stammered Wynn. *Damnit*, he was a Viscount! Why did he have to be so easily overwhelmed by a title?

He swallowed, then allowed the charming smile he had cultivated so well to spread across his face.

"Why, Your Grace, you would not betray me? I am, I admit, more accustomed to a simpler fare—but the soup course was truly delicious. I have not tasted better, I think, not even after visiting St. James's."

The Duchess of Axwick smiled, but Wynn was not fooled. There was a knowingness in that smile, which only a lady could have, and tension seeped into his shoulders.

In a softer voice so only he could hear her, she murmured, "My husband mentioned your dance with Lady Letitia a week ago. Do you not think she is quite beautiful? Not perhaps in society's eyes today, but I certainly think so."

Wynn's eyes drifted over to Letitia, now conversing quietly with the Duchess of Devonshire. There was something about her, as though a candle had been lit from within.

Something lower than his stomach contracted this time, painfully so. Wynn shifted in his seat and tried to think of the freezing cold baths he had endured when living at Redmont.

"Yes," he said quietly. "Very beautiful."

Letitia was like a piece of amber, wild red hair notwithstanding, she needed to be polished and placed in the proper setting for her beauty to be admired.

Almack's was no place for her. Forced into finery and dragged to be introduced to a stranger? No one would ever see Letitia in the best light there.

But here?

Letitia Cavendish was radiant, and no one else seemed to notice. Wynn swallowed. If he was not careful, he was at risk of making a fool of himself.

"I think she is probably one of the most beautiful young ladies in my acquaintance," Tabitha said quietly. "Of course, she is often underappreciated when in public. She does not perform in the way young ladies are expected to nowadays. But here..."

Her voice trailed away delicately, and all Wynn could do was nod. He could not take his eyes from Letitia.

"I had hoped her parents would join us, but then," Tabitha said delicately, "we would not see her at her best."

"I had thought her shy," he managed to say gruffly. "And yet, here she talks and laughs..."

"They call themselves 'the gang,' and never a

truer name was given," smiled Tabitha. "There are nine or ten of them, I believe, all who grew up together. They are more siblings than friends. 'Tis the only place she has the comfort to speak her mind on occasion."

Letitia was leaning forward, wide-eyed, a smile across her face.

"And then he said," Letitia offered, "my dear Madam, I am not the butler, I am your lawyer!"

The bottom end of the table erupted into laughter at her joke. Wynn stared at the bright eyes and joy on her face.

"Letitia, you must not say such things!" The Duchess of Devonshire giggled.

Wynn leaned forward, his desire to be close to Letitia so all-encompassing that he knocked into his plate and was forced to stretch with a yawn to cover the strange movement.

God's teeth, but this was ridiculous. He had seduced beauties and minor royalty. He should not even be interested in such a woman, and if so, he should have been able to charm her immediately.

But she did not want to be seduced—at least not by him. Something in her resistance fired his determination. The last three days had been torturous, raking over every memory, every encounter with her, however brief. But now he could see how much he had underestimated her. She was not the simple girl he had assumed.

She was still giggling at her own jest, but as she picked up her glass of wine, her gaze caught his.

The change was immediate. Laughter gone, a deep blush colored her cheeks, she appeared to wilt under his eyes, and she became physically smaller, desperate not to take up any more room than necessary.

It was astonishing.

"That," the Duchess of Axwick murmured, "is Letitia Cavendish. Never more afraid than when in the limelight."

Wynn smiled but did not say anything else. It was highly arousing, seeing the effect one look of his had on her. Her face was still pink as she sipped her wine, and when she placed the glass back on the table, her gray eyes darted over to him again.

He could feel himself become hard and shifted again in his seat. Was Letitia so unaccustomed to the admiring stares of gentlemen, for that was what it was, that she blushed?

Or perhaps she was fighting her own feelings for him. Wynn smiled at the thought. Perhaps she was flushed with desire, too.

Maybe she wanted him as much he was starting to want her?

"Ah, and here is another course," said Tabitha softly.

Wynn groaned. "Your Grace, how many

courses do you think there will be? If I do not slow down soon, I will be unable to keep this waistcoat on."

She smiled. "Three more, perhaps—or four? After this one, that is. Monty always requires his cook to do more courses than is good for any of us. You will have to accustom yourself if you are to come again."

Again? Wynn had not considered whether the honor of the invitation would be repeated, he was so fixated with Letitia.

He coughed as he looked down at another platter of food before him. This was ridiculous. He had to stop thinking—obsessing!—about Lady Letitia Cavendish.

Ignoring the fact she evidently had no interest in returning his advances, there were plenty of other young ladies who were desperate for his overtures.

Who did not want to be pursued by the most notorious rake of London?

If he was not mistaken, there were a few such ladies around this dining table alone. Their finery looked overdone, much like the meat before him. Too many diamonds, too much rouge, and a rather intriguing way of leaning forward so their breasts heaved toward him.

But they were not Letitia. Her gentleness, her awkwardness even, were more beguiling than any beauty ever had been.

Wynn looked to her end of the table. She was talking again with the Duchess of Devonshire, who laughed.

Suddenly, both of their heads turned to him, and Harry laughed even harder. Letitia did not. She merely stared coldly.

Wynn inclined his head, causing Harry to lean back in her chair in fits of laughter.

He wanted her. He wanted not just to bed her, but to make love to her. He wanted her to cry out his name as he plunged into her. He wanted to hold her close afterward, to kiss her, to hear all her thoughts, her worries, her hopes for the future.

He swallowed. *That was new.*

"To the Devonshires!"

A voice rang out at the other end of the table. Wynn jolted back to the moment and reached for his glass automatically.

"To the Devonshires!" the gentleman repeated with a smile. "Here's to their recent marriage, for a recent child, and against a recent end!"

There were chuckles around the table as they drank.

The Duchess of Devonshire raised an eyebrow. "My, my, Braedon, you are bold this evening."

Wynn glanced at the man who had made the toast.

"I seek only to please you, Your Grace," he

said, bowing his head.

She smiled. "I know, and I thank you. Our wedding was truly incredible."

"And we never saw it coming!"

Wynn did not see who had spoken, but their voice cut through the noise. He glanced at the Duke of Devonshire, but Monty did not seem concerned.

"Neither did I," he said with a laugh. "I was as surprised as you all were!"

The laughter became more relaxed, and Wynn leaned back in his chair. The meal was over, finally. Perhaps now he would be able to have an intimate conversation with—

"Of course, 'tis not the most surprising marriage of the season so far," Braedon said, interrupting his thoughts. "That surely has to be the Chester marriage."

The gentleman seated opposite Wynn nodded, but Monty did not seem so perplexed.

"I do not believe so," he said, his voice cold.

The table fell silent almost immediately. Monty's displeasure could be felt as well as seen.

After an awkward moment, someone spoke further down the table, and a small amount of chatter grew there.

Under its cover, Wynn murmured, "There is a story there."

Tabitha nodded. "The Duchess of Devonshire, Harry—Monty's wife—is the sister of

Josiah, the Duke of Chester. One has to remember, Wynn, we are all related somehow, when one reaches a certain level of society. Why, even you are a distant cousin of my husband, I think."

"I still do not fully understand. Why the sudden chill at the mention of the Chester marriage?"

"Ah, now there is a story," murmured Tabitha. "His bride is Honora, sister of the Duke of Mercia. She was abducted years ago, and when Chester encountered her, it was…well, at a brothel house. She was a courtesan there. That is how they met."

Wynn's eyebrows raised, but his smile did not disappear. He was a man of the world. He may even have visited the place.

The ways of the world and the ways of its gentlemen were, after all, quite different.

"'Tis still not the most scandalous thing that has ever occurred," he said quietly. "Nor is it the most scandalous way a husband and wife have met—at least not that I have heard."

"What say you, Wynn?"

Wynn started and looked around the table. What he had considered a private conversation with Tabitha had evidently been overheard, and now every pair of eyes were staring—some curious, some defensive.

He swallowed. He was a guest here, evidently an interloper. His pulse quickened, and his neck suddenly felt stiff. This was not the moment to speak the truth—but then he could hardly lie either, not if he had been overheard.

Wynn smiled. "I said, sir, that the Duke and Duchess of Chester's love story is not the most scandalous way a pair have ever met. Their health."

Raising the glass was a good idea. It propelled the entire table into drinking their health, not a single one of them willing to be bad-mannered enough not to join in.

"I do not agree."

Wynn looked down the table to see a gentleman he vaguely remembered being introduced to him as the Earl of Marnmouth. He was staring calmly with an eyebrow raised.

"You do not?" Wynn attempted to say lightly. *Damnit, how had he managed to spark a debate at the table of Letitia's close friend?*

Marnmouth shook his head. "I do not think it likely that people so unmatched can often fall in love. It rarely works."

"And yet, I am almost sure they can," Wynn found himself saying, almost to his own surprise. "It is rare, naturally, and if ever found, should be guarded. Such a connection is precious."

Silence fell after his words, his honesty perhaps out of place in good society. Wynn forced himself to remain quiet.

The Duchess of Devonshire rose in a rustling of silk. "I believe it is time for us to retreat. Ladies?"

There was a soft flurry of movement as the women around the table rose with her. Letitia determinedly avoided his eyes, despite Wynn's gaze following her.

When the door closed behind the ladies, Braedon laughed. "My God, Wynn, it almost sounded like you had someone in mind there! Any secrets you would like to share?"

Laughter echoed, but Wynn found his embarrassment had disappeared. Now that Letitia was not in the room, he had nothing to lose.

Even so, it was remarkably odd that a gentleman he hardly knew could make such an impertinent remark.

"Why do you laugh?" he asked mildly.

Most of the gentlemen stopped, and Wynn felt a little pride in his reputation. They cared enough about his opinion to ensure he was not entirely slighted.

"My dear, sir, you must understand your reputation as the greatest rake in town is well known," the gentleman opposite him said with a lazy smile. "You cannot seriously expect us to believe you are earnest about just one woman."

There were further chuckles at these words, and a prickle of irritation crept around Wynn's heart. Why could he not? Why could Letitia not be that woman?

Tiredness swept over him. His blood felt like lead, his bones as though he had ridden twenty miles.

Without a word, he rose.

"Dash it all, Wynn, you are not leaving so early?" Monty stared in genuine disappointment. "I have some fantastic cigars about the place, somewhere, if you are willing to stay."

Wynn bowed. "I, unfortunately, must leave, but I have felt welcome, Monty, and I would be grateful for a repeat invitation from you or your dear lady."

His host nodded.

"Gentlemen." Wynn bowed to the room, and as he turned to leave, he felt no regret. There had been nothing of interest in this room the moment Letitia had left it, and he was not going to waste an evening sitting with gentlemen who knew nothing beyond his rakish reputation.

"Thank you," he said curtly to the footman who opened the door into the hallway—and stopped as a door opposite him opened and revealed Letitia.

He stared for a moment, genuinely unable to speak. She colored, and her hands immediately clasped together.

"D-Do not let me detain you, sir," she managed, her eyes affixed on the carpet.

Wynn heard the door shut behind him. They

were completely alone. He could say anything. He could sweep her into his arms and—

"You are leaving?"

Wynn nodded. *Why in God's name was he unable to speak?* His eyes raked over her face. She did not look away. She wanted him, surely. Why did she resist it?

"I am leaving," he said, voice finally returning as he stepped toward the front door. "As are you. May I offer you the comfort of my carriage, Lady Letitia?"

If her cheeks had been pink before, they were crimson as she pulled on her pelisse.

"No," she said, far more firmly than he had been expecting. "No, thank you."

"My lady, the nights are dark, and you should not be walking home on your own." Wynn did not attempt to hide the concern in his voice. "Have your parents sent a carriage for you?"

He could almost see the thoughts in her mind. Desperate as she was to lie, she could not bring herself to do it.

"No," she whispered. "No, they have not. Thank you, sir."

What was he doing? As Wynn reached out to open the front door, any excuse to be close to Letitia felt like a good one.

"Here we are," he said as they stepped into the night.

His driver opened the carriage door, but it

was Wynn who reached out to help Letitia. She hesitated, took a deep breath, and placed her hand in his.

Magic sparked between them—heat and wonder, and something that pulled at Wynn's gut, which he did not understand.

Then it was over. He coughed and clambered into the carriage, closing the door behind him, and tapped on the roof to set them going.

Letitia was seated opposite, watching him carefully.

He smiled. "Do you make a study of my face for a portrait, Lady Letitia?"

She blushed prettily, gaze dropping to her hands. "I…I have heard all sorts of stories about you, Viscount Wynn. Some I cannot believe. Some I would rather not."

"Have you indeed?" For the first time, Wynn cursed his reputation. "And what are those stories?"

The intimacy of the carriage seemed to draw the same confidence he had seen at the dinner table.

"You seduce young ladies," she said, "and then you do not marry them. Is that why you want to pursue me, to ruin me?"

Wynn swallowed. This was an important moment, he knew, and one he would not get the chance to repeat. "I would never do that to you, Letitia."

"I have no reason to believe you. And I should not be in this carriage with you."

Something stirred in his stomach. "No, but perhaps I can give you a reason to take such a risk."

It took no time for Wynn to move and sit beside Letitia in the carriage. Her lips opened to express surprise, but they could not, for he crushed his lips onto her own, pouring all his passion, frustration, and desperation into the kiss.

He had expected resistance, even fear—but she responded with ardor like no other woman ever had. She leaned into him, her hands in his hair, pulling him closer, her tongue meeting his nervously but willingly.

"God, Letitia," Wynn breathed as they broke apart, his eyes searching hers.

She was staring as though he was an apparition, but instead of speaking, she pulled him close for another kiss.

Was it five minutes later, ten minutes, an hour? Wynn could barely tell. All he knew was the carriage coming to a halting stop and the door opening.

They broke apart, Letitia staring with a strange expression.

"Edward," she whispered.

Something painful and yet sweet jerked in his body as he croaked, "Letitia—"

But was she gone, like a breath on the wind.

"Letitia," he murmured, moving to follow her, so desperate was his need to be close to her—but he paused, hand outstretched.

She had walked up some steps, toward a large open door. In the blazing light pouring onto the street was the outline of a tall gentleman. Letitia was standing before him, head bowed.

Wynn leaned back with a sigh. If he was not mistaken, Letitia, despite being a young lady of two or three and twenty, was getting a telling off from her father.

CHAPTER FIVE

I F LETITIA WAS not careful, she would wander off the path at Hyde Park, distracted by the images flickering in her mind.

Viscount Wynn at dinner last night... Him speaking so honestly about love and couples who were meant for each other. How he offered her the use of his carriage so she could return home safely.

The viscount pulling her into his arms for the most passionate kiss that surely had ever occurred in the history of humankind.

She attempted to stay focused on her meeting with her best friend at Hyde Park.

So why did her thoughts continuously return to *him*?

She nodded at an acquaintance as they passed. The whole of society seemed to be out this morning, purposefully getting in her way as she tried to walk and not think.

Why had she let Viscount Wynn kiss her so wildly? His hands around her waist, his lips on hers. More than she could ever have dreamed of, more than she thought she would enjoy with a gentleman.

"You seduce young ladies, and then you do not marry them."

She swallowed and looked around for Mariah. She said she would be here, and if she did not arrive soon, it would be most impertinent. Being here alone, unchaperoned, was not a wise choice for a young lady.

"Is that why you want to pursue me, to ruin me?"

This was ridiculous, Letitia told herself. She was one in a long line of women with whom Wynn had enjoyed a little kissing in a carriage.

She wanted to be special to him, to be different—not just another lady foolish enough to acquiesce to his advances.

She wanted to be—what had he called it?

"It is rare, naturally, and if ever found, should be guarded. Such a connection is precious."

She dropped onto a bench and tried not to think. It did not help that she had hardly slept last night, her mind too awake after that intoxicating kiss.

"I am going to court you, Lady Letitia."

She swallowed again and tried to avoid looking at a pack of gentlemen walking by. She had never felt special before, but it was madness to think she could keep his attention for much longer.

It was one hour in his company. Perhaps less—yet she was obsessed with him. She could not deny, though she would never admit it, that when she had finally found rest last night, her dreams had been filled with Edward.

And those dreams had not halted at mere kissing. While in reality, it had been but ten minutes, in her dream, their carriage had rattled into the night uninterrupted.

In her dream, Wynn had taught her far more about lovemaking.

"Are you quite well, my dear?"

Letitia started. An elderly lady was standing before her, her face a picture of concern.

"I-I beg your pardon?" she managed.

"Your cheeks, dear," the old lady prompted. "You are red. Have you caught the sun? Are you seated because you can walk no further?"

Letitia raised a hand to her cheeks. "I thank you, but I am quite well. I am meeting a dear friend of mine here. Thank you for your concern."

The concerned woman seemed pacified as she walked away, but Letitia chastised herself for thinking such wild thoughts about Wynn. Genteel young ladies did not daydream about naked men, especially one who had no genuine interest in her.

But by God, she wanted him to. She wanted him to court her, but why would he?

When he had first arrived in town, Letitia had been taken with him immediately—a childish crush for which she felt ashamed, but that had not prevented her from delicately inquiring about him.

Edward Wynn liked beautiful women, women who could flirt and who would flirt back.

She did not fit into either category. The best thing was to completely ignore him. She would not see him, she would not seek him out, and if she was forced into the same room as him, she would remain at a cool and indifferent distance.

"That is the most impressively dull bonnet I have ever seen in my life."

Turning to see what idiot had spoken, she opened her mouth—and words utterly failed her.

Viscount Wynn stood there against the sunlight. "But the face underneath is far more beautiful."

Letitia silently begged her cheeks not to turn red, and yet they did not comply—as always.

"And that response is enough for me," he said with a grin. "My word, Letitia, I cannot decide when you are most delightful. When silent and blushing? Or when you are holding court with your friends who hang on your every word."

Finally, her legs obeyed, and she rose. Wynn was standing behind the bench, which stood between them as a protective barrier.

"Good morning, Viscount Wynn," she said stiffly, inclining her head rather than trusting her legs to carry her into a curtsey.

He bowed. She took her chance, strolling away at the greatest speed she could muster.

She was a fool to think it would work.

"Now, that is no way to treat a gentleman," he said as he caught up and fell into step with her. "Did you not wish to continue our conversation?"

"Conversation?" Letitia managed to say, her eyes darting around the park in a desperate attempt to find Mariah. "I do not believe we were having a conversation. You made a remark about my bonnet, and I left."

He chuckled. "I did not mean *that* conversation. I meant our conversation last night."

"I…I do not think we should…I do not want to…"

"Damnit, Letitia," Viscount Wynn said suddenly, reaching out and taking her arm, bringing her to a stop. "Why are you so proper?"

Her heart was thumping painfully, and his hand was burning her arm. *How had she managed to get into this situation—and in public, too!*

"I am a Cavendish," she retorted. "That is what we are, we are proper, and I will not allow you to besmirch me, sir. You may 'Wynn', as you so cleverly say, but my family has already won. We are at the top of the social tree, and I intend to keep us there."

Pulling her arm away, he allowed her to take a step.

"Good day, sir."

She started walking in the other direction. Perhaps Mariah was waiting at the gate—that would make sense. She would find Mariah, a chaperone and safety, which she had not expected to need.

She had been thinking about him, and he had appeared, as though he had known her thoughts.

"You know, I am starting to get the impression that you do not wish to converse with me."

Letitia sighed and slowed down. The viscount had caught her without any effort.

She swallowed. *How did one respond to him? How could she talk without embarrassing herself or giving the entirely wrong impression?*

It was hard to believe this was happening. In fact, it was exactly what she had hoped and feared. The two of them alone together.

She had to be grateful the encounter was in public. At least this way, he would keep his hands mostly to himself. If it had been a secluded part of the park, and she shivered at the thought, there was no telling what he would say to her.

Or what he would do to her.

"I am not here to converse with you," she managed to say, not looking at him. "I am here to meet a friend. As soon as I find her, you will have to leave us."

"Did you have a pleasant time at the Devonshires' dinner last night?"

Letitia almost laughed.

She swallowed. This was indecorous, and it would take only a snippet of their conversation to be overheard, and her reputation would be ruined.

"Yes, I had a pleasant time," she said a little more strongly.

His disappointment was clear, and it gave her a moment of unexpected pleasure. When was the last time a woman had rejected his invitation for further intimacy?

But it did not seem to humble the viscount. "Was that your father I spotted last night?"

She sighed and nodded.

They had reached one end of the park, and for one wild moment, Letitia considered running out of the gates and not stopping until she reached the safety of home.

But what was at home, except more rules—whereas here, she felt a tingle move down her spine each time she looked at Edward.

"It was my father," she said, turning around and continuing to walk. "I had not noticed the time, and when I did, I immediately left the Devonshires', but that was still too late."

"Letitia, you are a young lady, not a child."

"And he is my father," she said stiffly, a little

shocked at her own daring. "Ladies do not ever lose the caring eye of a gentleman, whether parent, partner, or progeny."

"There is far more to you than meets the eye, isn't there, Letitia? I do not think one in a thousand young ladies would even think that, let alone say it. And they call you a wallflower."

The word froze Letitia's heart. She stopped. "I would like you to leave me alone now."

"Why?"

She glanced up at the gentleman who was fast becoming the only man she could ever think of as a suitor.

"Because…" A quick glance about proved there was no one close, no one to overhear and get the wrong idea about what she was about to say. "Because…"

"Because you are a rake, sir," Letitia said, looking up into his dark eyes, wishing she could stare into them forever. "You are not to be trusted."

A gust of wind blew his dark hair, causing a spark of desire she did not understand.

"I would like you to trust me, Letty."

"You—you court many young ladies, and they all trust you," she breathed. "None of them last long, if the gossip of the *ton* is anything to go by."

"Well, you should not trust that gossip."

"I trust myself," she whispered. They were

intoxicatingly close now, and it felt wrong and deliciously right. "There is even talk you have…have ruined reputations."

"Would you like to find out firsthand?"

The invitation to further passion was intoxicating, but she would not allow herself to be overwhelmed. *She must not give in.*

"I am a joke to you, Viscount Wynn, and yet I have a reputation to maintain if I am ever to—"

"Ever to what?" he asked. "Ever to what, Letitia? Because if you want what I think you want, I may be about to offer that."

It was impossible to prevent her emotions from showing. Was he in earnest? Desire, panic, fascination, curiosity—it was not possible to untangle them.

"What say you?"

She did not know what to say—she was not sure she could remember how to speak. This was the longest conversation she had ever had with a gentleman in her life, and it was running away from her.

Taking a deep breath, she said, "I have nothing more to…to say to you, sir. As you have nothing but nonsense to say to me, I must say good day."

It was with a great effort of concentration that she stepped away from Viscount Wynn and started back toward the park gate. It was clear Mariah had forgotten their engagement, and the safest place she could be now was at home.

"Letty, wait!"

"What do you want from me?" She had not meant the words to be shouted, hurled at him as she turned on him in anger and desperation, but she was pushed to the brink. "What are you trying to prove? No gentleman speaks to me like this, they do not speak to me at all, and I do not trust you! What do you want?"

He looked a little surprised.

"I…" He swallowed, betraying a little hesitation of his own. "I do not know. I want to know you better, Letty, in every way."

His words did not seem to make any sense. "You said I am a wallflower. There is nothing else to know about me."

"You cannot be replanted? Somewhere else, in the sunshine, where you will thrive?"

She suddenly smiled, the image of the viscount as sunshine in her imagination. He was a foot from her now, but she had to end the conversation—if she was to maintain any sort of dignity.

"Good day, sir."

He caught her hand.

"Why," he whispered, looking down into her eyes with such fierce intensity, she gasped, "are you fighting this?"

All the breath was knocked out of her, her heart thumping wildly, her mind racing—and it was thrilling, a part of her wanting someone to see her in such a compromising position.

His hand was still entwined with her fingers, his other hand around her waist. Every nerve in her body was on fire, and try as she might, it was impossible not to think how few layers of clothing kept his skin from hers.

"F-Fight what?"

Viscount Wynn smiled. "This."

Without another word, he raised their hands and pressed hers to his chest right above his heart—which Letitia could feel pounding, even through the thick wool of his greatcoat.

She stared at their joined hands and then up at his face. It was almost impossible to believe, but there was no greater proof than his own heartbeat. *He felt something, too. His body was reacting to her just as she was reacting to him.*

Here she was, thinking she was alone in this confusing passion.

Her gaze dropped to his lips, and the need to kiss him rushed through her. They were alone here, no one would see. It would be a moment just between them.

His lips were only a few inches from hers.

"I do not understand," she murmured. "What does this all mean? What do you want from me, Edward?"

He rewarded her with a roguish grin, the kind that tempted her to do things she should never think about. And just as she thought he would finally kiss her…

"Good day, Lady Letitia."

Without another word, he walked away.

She stared after him, surprised her legs were still able to hold her up.

"Letitia, I do apologize, I got utterly caught up in a book and did not notice the time!"

Mariah was coming toward her, book in hand.

Mariah smiled as she reached her, slightly out of breath. "Did I miss anything?"

CHAPTER SIX

EDWARD SIGHED HEAVILY. "Are you absolutely sure that I have to go?"

His butler, Peters, smiled as he placed another silver platter on the dining table. "I would not dare tell his lordship what to do, naturally."

Edward sat alone at one end of the table with a glass of port in one hand and the damned invitation in the other.

It was from Lady Romeril, and it had been irritating him for the last three days. Covered in more gold leaf than he thought possible outside of Rome, the handwriting was in a delicate but old-fashioned style.

It greatly pleases Lady Romeril to extend an invitation to a ball at Twenty-Five Gardenia Place, London, on the seventeenth of this month.

RSVPs are not required. Lady Romeril looks forward to the pleasure of your company.

He sighed and placed the invitation down

beside his plate, taking a long sip of port. *RSVPs not required, indeed.* No, Lady Romeril would not even consider that someone who received her invitation would decline.

And to be fair, she was probably correct. He would be a fool not to go, even though the thought of another ball exhausted him.

Lady Romeril was one of the matriarchs of society.

He had heard she only held one ball a year in Bath, making it almost impossible for every debutante to receive an invitation.

Edward leaned back in his chair. The pain and pleasure of finding out whether you had been invited, whether your friends had—the gossips spreading the news of who had been left off the list this time…

It was sickening. Round they went, all of society in one giant circle waiting to be approved by each other. He was tired of it.

Now the only young lady on his mind was Lady Letitia Cavendish.

Just the thought of her made his blood boil, and he had to put the glass down carefully as thoughts of her overwhelmed him.

"Another glass, your lordship?"

God, every moment of his waking life was filled with Letitia; every one of his senses cried out for her. The way she smiled, the way she blushed—the way she kissed him in the carriage, the wild abandon he had not thought possible, the way she had wanted to kiss him so evidently in the park three days ago.

What did he want? *Everything.*

It was more than physical. More than anything he had experienced before. He had seduced Miss Keyford, enjoyed a brief dalliance with Miss Emma Tilbury—who had not?—but none compared to one kiss from Letitia.

"Are you quite well, sir?"

Edward jumped. Peters was standing beside him with the port bottle, concern across his features.

"Blast it all, Peters, cannot a man enjoy his thoughts?" he blustered, picking up his glass to allow the servant to refresh it. "Go on, leave me to it."

Lady Romeril's ball, he should think about leaving soon.

Would Letitia be there?

A cough made Edward start. Peters was standing in the open door with a greatcoat in his hands.

"Your carriage is waiting, your lordship."

Edward blinked. "My—my carriage? I did not order the carriage."

"No, sir, but I did," the butler said smoothly. "For your journey to Lady Romeril's ball. I am sure you will enjoy yourself when you get there."

Damnit, that was the trouble with clever servants.

It was why Edward had kept Peters on when his father had died; he needed someone who knew how to run a house.

"You are witty, are you not, Peters?" Edward said as he rose from his chair. "And yet, I am hardly dressed for—"

"I have the waistcoat and cravat right here, your lordship," said Jameson, appearing out of nowhere like a spirit in the mist. "I had the feeling you may not be quite adequately prepared for an outing at Lady Romeril's."

Edward smiled. His valet, new to the household and eager to please, looked like a puppy desperate to be picked up.

Peters caught his eye, and the two men grinned.

"You are circumspect, Jameson," Edward said gravely as he stepped into the hall and allowed his valet to remove his coat. "Peters, please send the carriage back for me at one o'clock."

"My goodness, sir," said the butler as Edward tried not to breathe as his cravat was tied. "So early?"

Edward nodded as his waistcoat was carefully buttoned up. "I do not believe this is going to be an exciting party, Peters, and I would rather be home for a good night's sleep. Thank you, Jameson."

There was a reason Viscount Wynn had not felt welcome in many of the best parlors in society. A mere viscount? But that would not deter him from making an appearance.

Was Letty invited?

She was a Cavendish. It was unlikely that Lady Romeril would have excluded her from the guest list. And that meant that his best chance of seeing Letty was right through those doors.

He stepped up into the house and was immediately accosted by Lady Romeril.

"Oh, my dear Viscount Wynn," she said with a false smile. "And I thought you would not come. What a pleasure."

"My lady," Edward returned her smile and bowed. "What an elegant gown you—"

"Yes, yes, that is all very well," Lady Romeril interrupted, her bad temper showing. "But I thought you were Prinny, dear boy, and I cannot pretend that compared to him, you are a bit of a disappointment. Who are you pursuing at the moment, by the way? I have not heard any gossip on you for what feels like an age. Ah—is that Prinny?"

Edward turned to see another gentleman walk up the steps, and not the Prince.

"What a disappointment you are, Lord Rust," said their hostess with a sigh. "Although I expect you hear that often."

"Only from my wife," smiled Lord Rust, good-naturedly, inclining his head toward Edward and walking by them.

After a few minutes of chatter with Lady Romeril and being warned not to ruin any of her guests' reputations, Edward was dismissed. He could leave now, and she would assume he stayed until three in the morning. But he should see if some familiar faces were in the card room before he disappeared.

He passed an open door leading to the dancing and saw a flurry of white gowns and gloves, and swallowed. If he knew Letitia, and he was not sure he did, she would be in there, watching the dazzling spectacle from a distance. Letty was not one to put herself forward, though she was easily the most beautiful woman he had ever seen. The more he looked, the more she eclipsed every other woman.

The moment he entered the card room, friendly faces appeared, Axwick, and a gentleman he had once been introduced to, the Earl of Chester.

Edward almost sagged with relief. Sane men, gentlemen with whom he could have a decent conversation for an hour and return home. No need for the carriage, he would walk—anything to be by himself again.

"Wynn," Axwick said with a grin as Edward dropped into the empty chair next to him. "I had not expected to see you here."

"No?" He inclined his head to Chester, who returned the courtesy. "Why?"

Axwick's grin broadened. "You are Edward, Viscount Wynn. Are you not inundated with party invitations and dinner engagements every single evening?"

He and Chester laughed without malice.

"There," said Chester impressively, throwing down his cards. "Now, tell me if you can that you have a better hand—I dare you!"

"I do not dare," Axwick said with a sigh, "and I still do not understand this game. Are you sure you are telling me the rules correctly?"

"Do you think I am cheating?" Chester asked in mock horror, and Edward chuckled.

Axwick shrugged. "I would not know if you were, and it matters little either way. More than thirty years without playing cards has left me at a permanent disadvantage, I fear."

"Did you see the news?" Chester looked at the pair of them with interest. "About the Earl of Liverpool?"

Axwick snorted as he pulled the cards toward him to reshuffle. "I do not believe he will be Prime Minister much longer, if you ask me."

The conversation washed over him. Politics had never interested the viscount.

Letty was probably a few feet away in the other room.

There was a pause in the conversation, and he took his chance to demonstrate he was still paying attention. "And is the scandal likely to be great?"

In that moment, a gentleman Edward did not know fell into the final empty chair at the table.

"I say, chaps, Mr. Jarvis is the name, and I am hoping you will be able to help me."

Edward glanced at Axwick, who was evidently as unimpressed at being addressed by a stranger as 'chaps' as he was.

Chester, however, was a gentleman with kinder sensibilities. "Good evening, Mr. Jarvis. How can we help you?"

The man had a mousey face and little hair and could have easily been any of their fathers.

"Why, 'tis the wallflower, of course."

Edward stiffened. "Wallflower?"

His word was quick, and all three gentlemen stared.

Mr. Jarvis nodded. "Yes, the wallflower in the other room. Who is she?"

"Is she exquisitely beautiful, with fiery hair and eyes like diamonds?"

Edward looked around for the gentleman who had spoken before he realized the astonished looks of Axwick, Chester, and Mr. Jarvis.

It had been him. He had spoken the thought aloud.

The embarrassed silence was not broken, and Edward felt, for the first time in a long time, the awkwardness of a person who had spoken out of turn in public. This was not like him; he was usually the charming one.

"I do not know, i'faith," Mr. Jarvis said, his nose scrunched up. "I would not say she is that pretty, 'pon my soul. Just a wallflower."

"That wallflower is probably Lady Letitia Cavendish," said Chester quietly.

Mr. Jarvis's stare now moved to him. "How can you know, you have not accompanied me to the other room to look at her!"

"Because," said Axwick in a voice which indicated the conversation would soon be closed, "in most social occasions, the wallflower is Lady Letitia Cavendish. A very *elegant* and proper young lady. Good evening, Mr. Jarvis."

Axwick began dealing out the cards, purposefully not placing a hand before the interloper—but Mr. Jarvis did not take the hint.

Instead, he laughed. "God, most social occasions? Well, if she is that desperate, I will stand up with her, to be sure—and see if I can get her lying down in a dark corner—arrggh, God's teeth!"

Edward's fist flew through the air without conscious thought and made contact with the stranger's nose with a satisfying crack. He found himself standing, chest heaving, fist aching, but a dull sense of satisfaction pouring through his veins.

Mr. Jarvis was lying on the floor. "Christ, what was that for? You want to tup her first? I don't mind waiting—don't let him touch me!"

Chester had indeed moved forward to hold Edward back.

"He is not worth it, Wynn," Axwick's voice said from behind him, but Edward's blood was boiling.

"He—he said," panted Edward, out of breath, his eyes narrowed and unwavering from the bleeding man. "He must not say such…disgusting things…"

But you wanted her yourself, a little voice reminded him.

"What in God's name is happening here?"

Edward turned. Several people had rushed into the room to see what the commotion was about, a gentleman had shouted out, and behind him was Letitia.

She stared as he shook his wrist, as though that would relieve him of the pain, and then her gaze moved to the man on the floor.

Shock was painted across her features, and Edward found himself overwhelmed by the bizarre hope that she knew it had been he who had defended her honor—coupled with the conviction that she should never hear Mr. Jarvis's disgusting words.

Pushing his chair aside, Edward walked away from the card table and the groaning Mr. Jarvis, and stopped before Letty. He offered her his hand, and she accepted it wordlessly.

As they walked out of the card room, it was

impossible to ignore the whispers.

"What in God's name—"

"Was that Viscount Wynn?"

"I never thought he would go for such a plain woman as Letitia Cavendish—"

"—willing to risk her reputation with—"

Edward's ears burned, but he did not stop. He wanted to get Letty as far away from Mr. Jarvis as possible, away from the gossiping tongues of Lady Romeril's guests.

It was an age until they reached the front door, and the cool air calmed him in a way nothing else could.

"And what," Letty asked nervously, "what that was all about?"

Edward sighed and leaned against the wall. The footmen had gone, thank goodness, and as no guests were leaving the ball early, there were no carriages in the street. They were alone— finally.

His voice was gruff when he finally spoke. "Where shall I return you?"

Letty blinked as though he had spoken another language.

"Where is your home? Where do you live?"

She pointed left, and in silence, they started to walk.

So many thoughts were whirling around Edward's mind, he was not sure whether he could speak coherently.

Where did one start? By punching Mr. Jarvis so publicly, he may as well have announced his intentions to the world—but Letty had not seen the altercation. She would have questions. Could he answer them honestly?

Did he want to?

After turning a corner, Edward eventually blurted, "I will not let anyone speak ill of you, Letty."

Even in the darkness, he could see that she had colored.

"Why?"

Edward stopped again.

Despite every instinct telling him to be silent, Edward took a deep breath. "I admit it. I care for you, Letty. I care for you more than I thought I could care for anyone."

The night seemed to ring out with his words, echoing down the empty street.

Letty swallowed. "Oh?"

His pulse was throbbing in his ears, but he had to press on. If he did not ask this question now, he would always be wondering, and there was no time like after he had punched a man for speaking ill of her.

"I have to know, Letty. Do you...do you care for me at all?"

She stared, her mouth falling open.

"I can feel the ridiculousness of my words," Edward said hastily, "and I hate myself for feeling so weak, yet I love that you have this effect on me. I-I do not know what to do with all these feelings, Letty."

She smiled, and it warmed him in a way that nothing else had. "I never thought Viscount Wynn would be asking anyone that, let alone me. Not the rake of the *ton*."

"Letty, I am in earnest," he said, taking a step toward her. "Do you care for me?"

There was a hint of despair in his heart. Why would a Cavendish risk her reputation, risk her heart, on a gentleman like him?

She nodded.

The relief was so great, Edward acted without thought. It took three steps until he was before her, and as she smiled, a wicked grin spread over his face. He pushed her slightly, so she stepped back against the wall. Then and only then did he give in to the desire roaring through his veins.

The kiss was unbelievable. Letty's breasts pressed against his chest, his hands on her hips, and his tongue plunging into her mouth, desperately taking all the pleasure he could.

And by God, she gave it to him. She kissed him just as passionately, just as desperately, as though they were the only real people in the whole world. As though nothing would ever tear them apart as long as they clung to each other.

Edward had never felt more alive, and his

body had never felt this way kissing anyone else. And it was Letty, Letitia Cavendish, the wallflower he and countless other gentlemen had undoubtedly ignored.

Where did it come from, this lust he had unlocked in her? Perhaps because no one else had ever touched her like this, kissed her like this, and Edward found himself getting even harder.

They broke apart when it was no longer possible to keep kissing without taking a breath.

"I would like to do so much more to you," he whispered.

Letty smiled, desire in her eyes. "And I want you to."

Edward's manhood jerked. There was no one else on the street—they would not be seen. He could taste the need in her, could tease her with his fingers until she cried out his name, and she would still be an innocent—in name at least.

"I-I should take you home," he managed to say in a strangled voice, "before I do something neither of us will regret."

CHAPTER SEVEN

LETITIA COULD BARELY stop her hands shaking, so she drew them together and tried to take a deep breath. Her lungs did not cooperate.

She swallowed, ignoring the pointed stares of those walking down Watling Street. This was reckless. She knew it and had never countenanced doing a thing like it before—but if she wanted a semblance of happiness, true joy, was it not incumbent on her to do something about it?

She could not continue waiting for happiness to arrive at her doorstep. This time, she was standing on happiness's doorstep. She had debated with herself, made up her mind, changed her mind—but if she did nothing, she would always wonder what if. What had Harry said?

"When you are in love, you will do anything."

"Good morning, Lady Letitia."

She jumped, for she had been in her own

private world. "G-Good morning, Mrs.—"

But the lady had already gone.

Letitia swallowed. She could stand here for a thousand years and still be no closer to potential happiness.

She was a Cavendish. Generations of men and women who took what they wanted without being asked—sometimes from other Cavendishes—had gone before her.

If she was going to live up to her name, like her father wanted her to, she needed to do something about her life. If she did not like it, all she had to do was change it.

Finally, she strode up the steps and knocked on the door.

It felt like hours until the door opened, and there stood a tall, rather grandfatherly looking gentleman in the soft green livery of the Wynns.

He peered around as though expecting to see someone with her.

"Yes, my Lady Letitia?"

She had hoped for some sort of anonymity and had not even crossed the threshold yet.

"You—you know me?"

The butler bowed. "Of course, my lady. I make it my business to be acquainted with the best of society, if only by sight and name."

Letitia hesitated. She should have expected it. One could not be a Cavendish and simply fade into the background all the time, even if she wished she could.

The butler was watching her with a kind look. "Did you knock for a purpose, my lady?"

"Y-Yes," she managed. "I...I wondered whether his lordship was in."

If the butler had been surprised at the rather unusual request, he did not show it. "I am not entirely sure if my master is at home, my lady, but if you will step inside, I will inquire."

The door was pushed open, and she caught a glimpse of a large hallway with a big, gold-framed painting on the wall. She swallowed. This was not what she had expected—in truth, she had not believed herself brave enough to even knock.

"Come in from the cold while you wait," said the butler gently.

She nodded and stepped across the threshold.

"I will be but one moment." The butler bowed once more and disappeared through one of the numerous doors leading off the hall.

Letitia looked around with a little trepidation.

So, this was the view that Edward—Viscount Wynn—saw every day.

As far as she knew, no other woman had come this far. From the stories she had heard, he liked to flirt with young ladies and make love to them in their own homes—and what their parents must have thought if they were ever caught, she could barely think!

The hall was bare, with few personal ornaments. She had never seen him in his natural setting before.

Whenever she did see him, it was all effortless charm and his desire to see women feel flattered, herself included. A spark of jealousy edged into her heart, but Letitia pushed it away decidedly. *It was not her place to judge what was in the past. She was his present. That had to be enough.*

Her eyes were drawn once again to the large gold frame on the wall and to the painting within it. Taking a breath as though she would spring a trap, Letitia stepped forward.

Her footstep on the stone echoed, but nothing else happened. She took a few more until she was standing before the painting, a family group.

On the right, an overbearing, stern gentleman. He had the same chin as Edward—Viscount Wynn—but none of the warmth. Seated beside him was a woman, beautiful but pale. She had Edward's eyes.

A young man stood behind his mother. There was no need to guess who he was.

She stepped back to take it all in and found that the overwhelming expression of all three of them was sadness. There was also something strange, something she could not put her finger on. There was something missing.

"Spotted anything interesting?"

The voice rang out behind her, and Letitia

turned around quickly, her heart thumping wildly. Edward was leaning against the opposite wall with a smile on his face.

Something painful contracted in Letitia's stomach. *My, but he was handsome—almost devilishly handsome, now she saw him in the comfort of his own home.* His cravat was only halfway tied, as though she had interrupted his valet, and she could see his chest, a few hairs poking through the top of his shirt.

She tried to swallow and speak at the same time. "Just now."

Heat rushed to her cheeks at the forwardness of her words—she had spoken without thought, and *that* was what had popped out!

She expected him to laugh or even be shocked. Plenty of her acquaintance would have been horrified to hear her speak in such a way. Edward smiled and did not move.

Letitia knew this had been a mistake. Coming here, before visiting hours, it was scandalous, and she should not have done it.

"What are you thinking?" He spoke calmly with a genuine look of interest on his face.

To prevent her truest thoughts from spilling out her mouth again, she said, "I was thinking about…about this painting."

Turning her back on him to look again at the family portrait, Letitia looked up at it. *Something about it was not right.*

Steps echoed in the hall as Edward joined her. "Yes, my parents."

He was not in a talkative mood, but Letitia had to fill the silence. "Tell me about it—about them."

Edward snorted. "There is not much to tell, I suppose. My father and my mother, one far kinder than the other, and I do not believe it would be difficult for you to tell which is which."

Letitia looked up again at the three figures. *No, even the painter had been unable to make his father's face kind.*

"My mother had wanted the painting," he said gruffly. "But she...she died before it was completed. She never got the chance to see it."

Letitia stared at the painting, unwilling to see the pain on his face. Yes, you could see it now. That paleness was not the fashionable tinge noble ladies wanted. It was far more than that.

"Consumption," Edward said into the silence.

There was still something a little odd about the painting. "You...you look young."

"I suppose I was," he said calmly, but she could hear the pain in his voice. "About twenty, I think from memory. That entire time is...it is a bit of a blur, if I am honest."

Instinctively, she moved her hand and took Edward's in hers. His were warm, more substantial than hers, but felt perfect.

No other gentleman had held her hand in this

way. If it had been anyone else, it would have felt a violation. He felt like home. As though she had been waiting for him all these years.

"It was a long time ago," Edward said quietly.

Then it struck her—what had been nudging at the back of her mind about the painting.

"Mariah."

"What did you say?" Edward looked at her quickly, and Letitia felt her cheeks burn.

"It is…well, Mariah. Your sister—"

"Adopted sister."

Letitia hesitated. She should have kept her mouth shut, but now she had begun…

"Something about the painting…I mean, 'tis a family portrait. But Mariah is not there."

He coughed and squeezed her hand. "It is a complicated story, Letty, and I would rather not tell it now."

She squeezed back. "Of course, Edward."

She gasped, dropping his hand and bringing both of hers to her face. Had she said his name aloud?

By the look of the grin on his face, she had.

"My word, Letty, we are moving quickly, are we not?" He was smiling more broadly than before. "Now, to what do I owe this pleasure?"

"I thought you might be interested in a walk."

Edward raised an eyebrow. "Without a chaperone? Are you willing to risk your reputation again? I am the greatest rake in town, as I think you have described me?"

She nodded. Nothing in the world was moving as quickly as Letitia's heartbeat. Edward's mocking smile faded and became a genuine one.

"Well, why did you not say so earlier? Peters!"

The butler opened a door and bowed. "Your lordship?

"Greatcoat, please," Edward said briskly. "We are going out. For a walk."

If the butler thought anything of the suggestion, he did not show it. He presented Edward with a greatcoat, and within a minute, Letitia was rushing down the steps with Viscount Wynn for a walk.

This was more than her secret hopes and dreams—but what would she say if they were seen unaccompanied in public?

"Now the question is," Edward said as they walked down the street, "not where we are going, but what you think you are doing, Lady Letitia?"

She glanced in fright, as though she had been caught doing something most irregular. "Doing?"

"Allowing yourself to be seen with me. It is wild of you."

She almost stumbled and was prevented from smashing her nose into the pavement by Edward's quick hands.

"Are you a mind reader, Viscount Wynn?"

His smile faded as she said his formal name. "No, why?"

"Because I was just thinking the same thing."

He stared for a moment and laughed. "Maybe I know you better than you think."

They turned a corner, and Letitia's heart skipped a beat. Anyone could be here, any of the gossips, her friends, family even.

"The more I know you," she said quietly, "the more I realize you are not the rake society thinks you are. If anything, you are quite the opposite."

"Oh?"

"And I do not think that you are the rake you think you are, either. All this, 'I always Wynn'. Does anyone else see through the façade?"

They were forced more closely together as a pair of ladies passed them, and Edward took the opportunity to speak in a low voice brimming with passion.

Letitia never wanted this walk to end.

"Letty, you see me in a way that no one else does."

"The fact you see me at all is far more than most people."

These revealing comments, from both of them—it must be love, surely?

"You saw the truth in the painting," he said quietly. "Anyone else just sees the prestige. No one else saw the misery, the loneliness. But you did."

She heard the pain in his words. "Your mother?"

He nodded. "Both she and I...I will not say suffered, for we had more than most. A home, warmth, food, clothes, all the practical things—wealth. I am sure there were many who knew us and envied our luxuries of life. But without love, without a feeling of safety, what use is gold?"

"He—he did not..."

"Oh, no," Edward assured. "Never physically violent, my father. No, he could do plenty of damage without laying a finger on any of us. I suppose I should not blame him so harshly. He could only care for us how he was raised. He knew no different, but by God, I wish I did."

Letitia swallowed down her questions. He was right; anyone who looked at him would assume he had known only comfort and love, but he had not. He had suffered because his own father had not known how to love. So, did Edward?

As she opened her mouth, someone shouted after them.

"Hie there—it is you! Letitia!"

Letitia halted and looked to the other side of the street, and smiled to see Mariah Wynn, spectacles and a harassed look on her face.

It took her four attempts to cross the street

with the carriages racing by so quickly, and Letitia looked at her companion. There was coldness in Edward's face.

"Ah, it is you," said Mariah as she finally reached them.

The two ladies dropped into curtseys, and Edward bowed his head. Before Letitia could explain, Mariah spoke again.

"So, you are walking with him. In public, too. Why?"

Letitia swallowed and looked between the adopted siblings with concern. "Y-Your brother?"

"Adoptive brother," muttered Edward under his breath.

"As if you would let me forget it," Mariah hissed.

The tension was unbearable. Letitia cast about desperately for words that would not make the conversation even worse than it already was.

"We were going for a walk," she said quietly. "And you, Mariah, were you going somewhere special?"

But Mariah did not oblige. "I warn you, Wynn, if you are not careful with Letitia's reputation, you will not only have her parents to answer to, but you will be forced to contend with me."

Letitia blushed, but her obvious discomfort was not enough to distract the siblings.

"And you believe I would be so careless with

it?"

Mariah snorted. "I know you, Wynn, and I know your ways. I do not wish to see my friend hurt."

"I am going to take better care of her reputation than I have my own," said Edward flatly, glancing at Letitia, who wanted the ground to swallow her whole. With a curt nod to Mariah, he pulled Letitia away, and they continued down the street.

It was impossible not to ask. "Edward, why are you two always at odds with each other?"

Edward snorted, and it was only then that Letitia saw a likeness between the adopted pair. "Mariah sees offenses where there are none—she seeks offenses where there are none! I have learned to ignore her."

Letitia hesitated, opened her mouth, and decided against it. Nothing could be gained by contradicting him, and Mariah did have a certain way about her that made her unpopular in some circles.

"Your friend is concerned about you and your reputation, and that does her credit," he said abruptly. "Though her concern is unwarranted. I told you. I want to court you."

She smiled, heat washing through her body, but before she could reply, she was interrupted.

"Wynn—hie, Wynn!"

"Are we to be continuously interrupted?" she

breathed, and Edward grinned before he welcomed Abraham Fitzclarence, Viscount Braedon.

"Ah, I see you are with the beautiful..." Viscount Braedon's voice trailed away as he turned to the young lady beside him and was evidently astonished to see her.

Letitia's head lowered with shame. No one expected her, the wallflower of society, to be in the company of such a handsome and charming man.

"...beautiful Lady Letitia Cavendish, the woman with diamond eyes," Viscount Braedon said jovially.

Letitia had expected worse, but what surprised her more was the look of embarrassment on Edward's face. *Was he that ashamed to be seen with her?*

"That is what you called her, is it not?" Viscount Braedon said with a cough, as though wishing desperately he had never embarked on the conversation. "At Lady Romeril's ball, before you punched Mr. Jarvis? That is what I heard."

Letitia stared at Viscount Braedon in astonishment. *Diamond eyes? Had Edward said that about her—and to a gentleman at a ball, where anyone could hear him?*

Edward coughed. "Those were the words if I recall."

Viscount Braedon grinned. "I did not realize

you were courting, man, but now I understand the fist."

"Fist—Edward," Letitia said, realization finally dawning, "it was—it was you who punched Mr. Jarvis?"

Viscount Braedon was suddenly aware that he was no longer required in the conversation. "I will see you at the club then, Wynn. My lady, your servant."

Letitia barely noticed him go. "Edward, you…you punched a man because of me? Why?"

"I would have done it for any young lady of my acquaintance, the way Mr. Jarvis was talking," he said heatedly, but his voice calmed as he continued, "though I took pleasure in defending your honor. I should have told you."

Reeling from this new information, she said, "Are you…are you going to attack any other gentlemen in my name?"

"Probably not, although I make no promises."

A church tower rang out, and Letitia bit her lip. "I should be back home, Ed—Viscount Wynn," she amended hastily as someone passed them. "For visiting hours, you see. My father will require it—unless you would like to return with me and meet—"

"I have some business to attend to," Edward said quickly. "What a shame."

Letitia hesitated. *Surely if he were courting her*

in good faith, he would want to meet her father at the first opportunity?

"You know, both of our friends want what is best for us," she said as she curtseyed her goodbye.

Edward bowed and smiled wryly before she turned to go. "Oh, Letty. Until I met you, I did not even know what was good for me."

CHAPTER EIGHT

A BITTER WIND blew, and Edward pulled the lapels of his greatcoat closer as he sat in darkness. Anyone who saw him would think him an absolute fool—or worse, a complete vagabond. What did he think he was doing, sitting out here on the steps of a house as though he had lost all his reason?

Perhaps he had. Perhaps that was why he could not bring himself to go inside, or even attempt to look through the windows.

"...unless you would like to return with me and meet—"

Edward snorted. *Well, honestly, what had she been thinking?* He was not the sort of gentleman that a young lady wanted her parents to even know existed—much less admit she was courting.

Letitia was so innocent.

Not him. Not when his body was raging for release, and he desperately wanted to stride into this house, find Letitia wherever she was, rip off her clothes, and make love to her.

He rarely ever met the parents of the women he bedded—and even on the rare occasion that he was introduced, they never had any idea he had ravished their daughters.

Something painful contracted in his stomach, and he stood, no longer able to bear the cold. Letty was different. Always a wallflower, that is what she considered herself—when all he could do was marvel at her beauty.

There was no one less suited to being a wall-flower in the world. All she needed was a little attention, and see how she had blossomed! She turned up at his house yesterday, asking whether he would take a walk with her.

He had wanted to take far more than that.

God's teeth, but it was cold.

It did not make any sense. Anyone who took more than five minutes speaking with Letty, once she had overcome her shyness, would have seen she was the image of perfection.

How was he the first to notice it?

Thoughts of Letty flooded warmth through his body, though his fingers were still cold. Edward blew on them as he paced up and down outside her home.

He should be grateful he was the first to notice it. Just think who could have taken advantage of her, married her even before he had been introduced to her at Almack's.

He sighed, watching his breath billow. He had to do something. He was not going to stand out here all night.

Screwing up his courage, he strode up the steps, reached out—and did not knock.

This was foolish beyond belief. This was Letty's home, and her parents would be in there. How would he explain a nine o'clock evening visit?

Edward's hand fell. Why was he so charming to every woman except the one he truly felt something for?

He walked heavily down the steps and leaned against the railings. What was he to do?

"Who is there?"

Edward froze and turned slowly on the spot. A Thames River police official, dressed in the newfangled garb of the docks, was striding toward him.

"Good evening, sir, and how may I assist you?"

The official bristled. "I think it is more likely can I do something for you! What are you doing, if I may be so bold as to ask?"

Edward hesitated. He did not like lying, and there was usually a way out of a situation without doing so. Could he find one now?

He winked at the official and jerked his head back up the road. "Ah, sir, a gentleman never tells."

The official hesitated.

"I do not believe we have been introduced," the official said slowly.

Edward bowed, lower than he normally would, but it could not hurt. "Edward, Viscount Wynn, at your service."

It was enough. When he straightened up, he could see the official's eyes were wide in genuine astonishment. He had met one of society's greatest rakes on the streets of London.

"I see I am known by reputation, if not by sight," he said breezily. "Now then, officer, you would not ask me to betray and ruin a lady's reputation after enjoying an evening...conversation."

He did not wink again—he did not need to. The lingering pause was just enough to convey his meaning, and as he had hoped, the official was a man of the world.

"I quite understand, sir, and I do apologize for delaying you on your way home," the man said smoothly. "I expect you are tired after all your...conversation."

Edward almost laughed aloud. "Thank you, sir. I will wait here a moment to catch my breath after such vigorous...conversation. Good evening."

The official nodded. "Good evening, sir."

Edward watched until he could no longer

make him out in the gloom and dropped onto the steps with relief. What a night to be caught— *almost.*

Well, if he did not have the gumption to walk up these damned steps, knock on that door, and introduce himself at this late hour to Letty's father, perhaps he did not deserve her.

The moonlight broke through the clouds, and the street was filled with light. Edward sighed. *No, he was probably not good enough for Letitia—but despite that, he wanted her.*

Moving quickly, he rose and went around the side of the house and found what he knew would be there—a door to the kitchen.

A footman opened it warily. "Yes?"

Edward smiled. Now to bring out the charm again. "You look like a man of the world, sir—I am here to see the lady of the house."

The footman blinked. "Lady Cavendish?"

Edward's smile became a little more brittle. Only he could have found the idiot of the house. "No, the younger lady of the house—Lady Letitia."

The footman took a careful look, a grin creeping over his face. "Oh, are you?"

Edward nodded. Time to speed things up a bit. "A guinea for entry, my good man, and another for your silence?"

The footman hesitated, but the production of one of the promised coins before his eyes tipped the balance.

"Go on then, sir," he said magnanimously. "Do you know your way?"

Edward shook his head as he stepped into the kitchen, which was blindingly bright after the murk of outside.

"No, but I will find my way. Now, remember—your second guinea is for silence, and it will be yours tomorrow should all go well."

The footman inclined his head and pointed. "That way, sir."

Edward felt like a common thief as he crept along the servant's corridor, the pounding of his heart echoing as he opened a door into the hall. There was a single candle ablaze in a mirrored stand by the front door.

Now what? His pulse was so loud, he was astonished no one else had heard it.

Closing the door behind him, Edward leaned against the wall. Every sensible thought told him to go back, but he could not.

He had to see Letitia.

He stepped forward and tried a door. The room was empty and in darkness, but he could make out enough to tell it was the breakfast room. Returning to the hall, Edward tried not to laugh with the bizarreness of it all.

There were four other doors in the hall. One more try, and he would find his way back down to the kitchen.

His hand closed on the door handle, and when he opened it, light poured out into the hallway. Edward hesitated. All three Cavendishes could be inside this room. Was he ready for the consequences of his actions?

"Mama?"

Edward froze. That was Letty's voice; he knew it anywhere.

"Papa, is that you?"

He let his breath out slowly. So, neither of her parents were in there with her. She was alone.

Edward stepped through the door and closed it behind him.

The most incredible sight met his eyes— Letty in a pale white gown, seated near the fire, which illuminated her fiery red hair beautifully. She was a picture of perfection, and most importantly, she was alone.

"Edward!" Letty stared aghast, as though she had seen an apparition. "What—what are you doing here?"

Edward ignored her question. "Where are your parents?"

She smiled at his evasion. "Out this evening, at Lady Romeril's for dinner. They were otherwise engaged when the invitation for her ball arrived, and they felt they had to make amends. Why?"

The tightness around Edward's chest disappeared. *So, they were alone—truly alone.* Moving closer and sitting beside her on the sofa, he swallowed. He would have to play this carefully.

"Would you believe me if I answered honestly?"

Letty smiled, though there was a look of concern in her eyes. "Can you answer honestly?"

Edward laughed and knew he was falling in love with her. By God, but she was everything he could have ever wanted: witty, pretty, and not afraid of him. And Letty was afraid of everything. But, he, she trusted.

It was the most incredible sensation. He had never traded much in honesty with any of the other young ladies he had wooed, but the thought of lying to Letitia made him feel physically unwell.

"I wanted to see you," he said honestly. "I...I missed you."

Even in the flickering firelight, he could tell she blushed at his words.

"But Edward, it has only been a few days since we last saw each other."

"Too long," he replied, wondering whether now would be a good time to move closer to her on the sofa.

It was not.

"All those pretty phrases, very well put together," Letty said with a smile a little too knowing for his liking. "Almost as though you have used them before."

Shame flooded through Edward that he could not stem. He had used them before, but he had never felt them—never actually meant them.

This did not feel the right time to admit it. Edward coughed. "What do you think of me, Letty? I would welcome your honest opinion."

She stared for a moment, rose from the sofa, and sat on the opposite sofa before answering.

"I think you are a handsome devil," she said, "and someone I should stay far away from."

"You know, I rather like that description."

Letty laughed. "I thought you would. Rather proves my point, doesn't it?"

He had to be close to her; no matter what their conversation, it felt stilted being so far apart. Not taking his eyes from her gray ones, Edward joined her on the other sofa.

"I am sure that you could reform me if you wanted."

"I am not sure whether I can."

"But I want you to."

He had never been so vulnerable with a woman before. But Letty was worth it. She was worth it all.

She stared, the fire lighting up her hair until she finally spoke in a low voice.

"I may be bored with being a wallflower and never the bride, but I do not think it likely you will be meeting me at the top of the aisle any time soon."

He gazed at her, and for once, she held his stare. "Is that truly how you think of yourself? Always the wallflower and never the bride?"

She laughed, and Edward could hear the tinge of sadness. "Well, I am! I am not going to pretend to be what I am not."

"And are you happy?"

"I am at this moment," she said eventually.

"We are all alone in this house, with no one to prevent me from doing anything I like, and I am here talking to you—the greatest rake in London, your words! That has to count for something."

"Well, of course I hate being considered a wallflower," she admitted quietly. "Is there anything more upsetting than being laughed at because you find it difficult to talk to people?"

"You have no trouble speaking with me."

"Yes, but only because I know you would never consider me...you know. That way. Not really."

Something stabbed into Edward's heart. "What way?"

Letty colored, suddenly aware she had been too honest. "You know. Please do not make me spell it out for you."

"Tell me," he urged, though he had a suspicion, and it was one she confirmed.

"The way you would consider a woman you

could make love to, Edward. And that is not me."

Hearing his name on her lips was enough to push him over the edge. "Letty Cavendish, I have only ever seen you that way."

He moved swiftly, pouring every feeling he had for Letty, even the ones he did not understand, into the kiss that he pressed upon her lips.

CHAPTER NINE

THIS WAS NOT happening—it could not possibly be happening. Letitia was overwhelmed with sensations, the heat of the fire on her back, the heat of Edward's lips on hers, the heat between her legs, which she did not understand.

It was too much, and yet, she could not ignore the feeling of his lips on hers, the sensation of his arms around her, pulling her closer.

It was real. Edward, Viscount Wynn, was kissing her and wanted to make love to her.

His tongue teased her lips, and she opened for him, desperate for the sensation, and she moaned in his mouth.

Letitia wanted to lose herself in him—but surely this was not right, it could not be.

She knew his reputation. This was only going to end one way, and that was with the loss of her reputation. Her parents were not even in the house, and she was utterly vulnerable. How had he managed to get in?

Edward pulled away, lust in his eyes, but concern across his face. "Letty, what is wrong?"

This was not the best time to voice her growing concerns that he was far more interested in what was underneath her gown than hidden in her heart.

If she did not speak now, would she ever be truly honest with him?

If speaking meant ending this incredible encounter, then was it truly honorable at all?

"I-I wanted to say," she stammered, "I know I am just another notch in your bedpost—well, mine, I suppose, as this is my house—but Edward, you—you matter to me and—"

"You are not," interrupted Edward, "just another notch in my bedpost—you were never that, and you never will be. Do you think that little of yourself?"

His words were kind, concerned. It made it all the more difficult for Letitia to meet his gaze as she spoke.

"Well…that is what you think of me."

Edward actually leaned back slightly at her words, eyes wide with shock.

Oh, you stupid fool, Letitia thought quietly. *He will disappear now, and you will never see him again. Never. That was your chance, perhaps your one chance to experience what it is to make love—to truly be one with a gentleman—and now your chance is gone.*

Edward sighed, then dropped suddenly to his knees on the floor, prostrate at her feet.

"Edward!"

"I feel more passionately about you, Lady Letitia Cavendish," Edward said calmly, "than anyone else I have ever met. Yes, I have bedded other women. I am not going to lie about it, Letty, but I will tell you this. I have *bedded* other women. I have not made love to them. I want to make love to you."

She could barely speak. "There is no difference."

"Yes, there is, and I should know," he said calmly, still on his knees. "Trust me. Let me show you."

She wanted him in a way she had not known existed before tonight.

"What is the difference?" she whispered.

Edward smiled, and it was wicked and delicious. "Try not to be too loud."

Letitia could not help but laugh. "I do not think I have ever been accused of being too loud before in my—oh!"

He had placed a hand on each of her knees and moved them apart with a hungry look on his face.

"What are you going to do?"

"Something I have wanted to do for a long time. If you want me to stop, say. But you won't."

His words did not make any sense, and she was just as bemused when Edward leaned forward, raised the skirts of her gown, and lifted them over his head.

"Edward, what are you—Lord!"

Letitia had never blasphemed, but she had never needed to before. Edward was slowly kissing up her inner thighs, and it was having such a wonderful effect on her body…

"Edward?" she whispered, hardly able to watch his head move under her skirts but knowing, all of a sudden, where he was going. "Edward, I—oh!"

His tongue had reached her secret place, and she spasmed at the intensity of the sensation—it was pure pleasure, but it was more than that. The intimacy of it all, his face right…*there.*

She grasped the edge of the sofa as Edward's tongue made a thorough exploration of her. Now she knew what he meant about being loud—the last thing she wanted was a servant running in here.

She leaned back and tried to breathe, but the teasing kisses were driving her wild.

"Edward, yes," she whispered just loud enough for him to hear. "Oh, yes, oh—!"

A climax made her entire body clench and rock as his tongue delved deeply into her.

When Edward resurfaced, a broad smile on

his face, Letitia hardly knew where to look.

"I…I had no idea," she panted, "such pleasure could exist."

"'Tis only the beginning."

It was impossible to breathe. "Beginning?"

Edward grinned. "Take me to your bed-chamber."

SHE HAD NEVER felt anything like that—but once her innocence was lost, it would be lost forever.

Was she ready to lose it all to Edward?

He made her feel such incredible things, but only ten minutes ago, he was admitting the countless women he had bedded.

He was a rake, pure and simple. If anyone ever found out—if the news was ever public …

No one would permit her to enter their homes. She would never be invited to another ball again.

Letitia looked down at Edward and smiled as her heart softened. Wallflower or not, she was in love with him.

Staying at home forever was not the end of the world. She was a Cavendish. She would go to the country and live a life of leisure, safe in the knowledge that she had, finally, been made love to by a wonderful man.

"Well?" Edward prompted.

She smiled. *What was it that Harry had said?*

"I had to, Letitia, I just had to. It was impossible for Monty to see me any differently unless...unless I took drastic action."

Unable to trust her voice, she nodded.

Edward jumped up, pulling her to her feet. "Quietly now."

He pulled her to the door, Letitia barely understanding how her legs could support her after so recently spasming with pleasure.

Edward peered out.

"Can you see anyone?" she whispered.

He glanced at her with a smile. "No. Come on!"

Opening the door, they crept into the hall, which was indeed empty. Letitia almost laughed aloud but stopped herself. This was insane—she had never done anything like this.

The stairs were right beside the door, and they almost ran up to the next landing.

"This way." Letitia pulled him toward her bedchamber.

The moment they shut the door, Edward pushed her up against it and kissed her deeply. She threw her arms around him—he was hers, and she would have him for at least this night. Perhaps longer. *Was this, perhaps, the prelude to a proposal of marriage?*

"I want to see you come again," Edward

whispered as he kissed her neck.

Letitia hesitated. "Come?"

He chuckled as he nuzzled her décolletage. "Climax, orgasm. I have so much to teach you, Letty, and I cannot wait. But first…"

One of his hands holding her so firmly against the door now descended, pulling up the skirts of her gown, and Letitia stared in wonder until her eyes widened with pleasure.

His fingers were where his mouth had just been, and they were working a similar rhythm— soft but steady, driving her absolutely wild.

"Edward," she moaned, but he captured her words in his mouth and kissed her hard, keeping her quiet and teasing her even more as his fingers quickened the pace.

How long was it—five minutes, more? Letitia could not tell. Soon, she was exploding around his fingers, her body tensing and shuddering as the pleasure once again overwhelmed her.

"I did…I did not know of this love," she panted, gazing into his eyes as Edward smiled. "I could not have imagined such feelings, such sensations."

His smile broadened. "And we are not there yet."

Allowing her skirts to fall, his fingers moved to the ribbons holding her gown together, and panic suddenly rushed through her body.

"Stop!"

She had not shouted, but the word was clear, and Edward immediately stepped back and broke the connection.

"Are you—I am sorry, did I hurt you?" The concern in his eyes was genuine. "Letty, I should not have rushed you, I apologize—you must forgive me if..."

Edward's voice trailed away as he stared, clearly uncomfortable and unsure what to do next.

"I-I do trust you," she said. "But this...this is all new to me, Edward. We need to go slower."

He nodded. "You are in control, then. You take off what you are comfortable with."

She had never had many conversations with her female friends about lovemaking. All she had heard whispered by the matrons of society was about pain, discomfort, and allowing the gentleman to do what he needed to do.

But this care, this consideration... She had expected thrusting and pain, and a little moment of joy for herself.

Hearing Edward say aloud that he handed the control to her—that nothing would happen unless she was comfortable...

He clearly cared about her. *Perhaps more.*

But she could not think of that now. Her body was aching for more pleasure, and she would succumb, she knew she would. But not yet.

Letitia slowly pushed Edward back until he reached the bed. A slight shove was enough to make him sit down.

His smile froze as she carefully, without taking her eyes off him, started to pull gently at the ribbon holding her bodice together.

"Christ, Letitia," he groaned under his breath. "The things you do to me…"

Just seeing the reaction in his eyes, seeing him fidget, knowing he wanted to touch her but denying him that right…

It was glorious. It made her feel the most powerful woman in the world.

"Letty, you are the most beautiful woman."

She allowed her gown to fall to the carpet slowly.

By the time she had stripped off her underslip, Edward had ripped off his own clothes and was sitting patiently. Any embarrassment in her nakedness was gone.

"Are you ready for me?" she asked, hardly knowing what she was doing.

Edward groaned. "Put me out of my misery."

Letitia stepped forward, out of reach of his questing fingers. He moaned again, and she giggled, shushing him.

"The only way to shush me," he growled, "is to kiss me."

He moaned as she kissed him. The thrill of experiencing every sensation at once: the feel of his chest on her breasts, his arms around her, his manhood hard and throbbing and pressed into her thigh—it was all too glorious.

His wandering tongue had found her breasts, and in one movement had captured her nipple in his mouth. The teasing, wet sensation, along with the rubbing of his manhood against her, was almost enough to make her explode again.

Edward stopped and looked up at her, eyes wide. "Are you ready?"

She nodded.

He lifted her as though she weighed nothing, laying her down on the bed and nestling between her as though he belonged there.

Perhaps he did. Perhaps every moment of their lives, even the painful ones, had been leading up to this moment, this second where they loved each other.

"Ready?"

Letitia nodded and almost cried out when he entered her—but there was tightness, not pain. Edward held himself there, deep inside her, and she smiled nervously.

"Is this—is this it, then? We have made love?"

"Almost."

He drew out of her, almost completely, and thrust into her. Letitia gasped as a rush of delicious pleasure flashed through her.

"Again," she whispered, leaning up for a kiss.

And she got what she wanted. Edward built

the rhythm carefully, his lips possessing her, worshiping her, as he moved in and out of her faster and faster. Letitia barely knew where he ended, and she began, it was an experience so intimate.

"Edward," she began, breaking their kiss.

He looked deep into her eyes, and she came, exploding around him. Then he found his pleasure.

When it was over, he fell into her welcoming arms.

CHAPTER TEN

OW LONG HE had slept, Edward did not know. Time stood still.

His rest had been deeper than he expected, considering it was not his bed. While that was not entirely unusual—after all, a rake could get tired and decide not to return home after a session with a new conquest—and this was a new bed for him.

Edward smiled and looked over at the woman lying next to him, still fast asleep.

Lady Letitia Cavendish.

Far more wild and just as sweet as he had thought—and now those estimations were confirmed in the most delicious way.

"Christ alive, Letty, put me out of my misery."

Edward shifted onto his back, eyes still fixed on her.

He swallowed and forced down the rush of desire that swelled from his manhood to his heart. He should let her sleep. He had worn her out, after all, and she had earned her rest.

Edward had always considered himself to have an eye for the ladies, able to pick from a crowd who would allow him a kiss by the staircase, and who would be happy to lead him up those stairs by the hand.

But he could never have predicted what Letty had underneath those plain and boring gowns.

Why did she never want to put herself forward? If any gentlemen knew how wild and free Letty was, well, she would already be a married woman, surely.

God, he was getting hard thinking about her.

His gaze traced the flow of her fiery hair that fell like a waterfall down her back and resisted the urge to reach out and touch her.

All that beauty, and she was not proud or conceited. Letty was unlike anyone he had ever met. He could search the entire empire and never find another to match her.

Edward looked around for a clock, but he could not see one. His clothes had been dropped to the floor in the heat of passion hours ago and could not be reached without disturbing Letty.

The curtains were pulled across the high windows, but a crack of light poured through. It must be morning, just past sunrise.

Edward bit his lip. When he bedded a lady, she knew not to expect to see him in the morning. He always intended to be gone before sunrise, all the better to avoid seeing parents, servants, and being spotted leaving the house.

Awkward conversations had only been experienced twice, and even now, he winced. That moment discussing the weather with Lord Cramer's butler, and that uncomfortable invitation to breakfast from Mrs. Pickering.

Never again.

But something pricked at his conscience as he glanced once more on the sleeping Letty. This was more than a mere bedding. They had made love. And after all, Lady Romeril's dinners were notorious for being too long, and in many cases, she offered beds to her guests so they would not have to leave at four o'clock in the morning.

Letty's parents may not even be here. There was no chance of running into them on the stairs, but what about the servants?

Perhaps he should leave now. That seemed safest.

Just as Edward decided to, Letty turned in her sleep, coming to rest curled in a ball on her side with her breasts uncovered and a smile on her face.

God, she was beautiful, but she was more than that. She made him want her attention, her conversation, her laughter.

Last night gave him intense pleasure, but perhaps far more importantly, he gave her such pleasure. There had been a deep connection between them.

"Edward?"

He started, thoughts interrupted.

"You are meant to be asleep," he murmured, finally giving in to temptation and reaching out to touch her. "Go back to sleep, Letty. I will be here when you wake up."

How could he leave her now?

A soft smile spread across her lips, and her eyelids fluttered sleepily—then snapped open.

"You are—you are not a dream?" Pink tinged her cheeks.

"Good morning, my darling."

The words felt natural. He had never spoken them to anyone else in his life, but they poured out from a place of deep affection.

"You…I…I am not wearing anything!" Letty pulled the bedcovers up to her neck.

There was only about six inches between them, and he closed it quickly, searing a kiss on her lips fueled by the memories of their passion hours ago—and the desire to repeat them.

Letty returned his ardor, crawling into his arms. After several minutes of passionate kissing, they broke apart.

"Not how I imagined I would wake up," she whispered, her fiery hair a halo around her.

He grinned. "But exactly how I wanted to."

Letty smiled shyly, her gray eyes sparkling.

"I-I cannot believe what we did last night, Edward."

"Oh, I can…"

"Shush!" She placed a hand over his mouth as she collapsed to his side in fits of silent giggles. "Edward, my parents are two rooms down!"

The mention of her parents sobered him. "Nonsense, they dined with Lady Romeril. You said so yourself."

"Yes, I did, but they never accept her offer of overnight hospitality. They always come back here."

Without another word, she snuggled against him and rested a hand on his chest above his heart—which was now starting to race. If Letty was right, Lord and Lady Cavendish were home.

Not two people he wanted to meet. What if Lady Cavendish was in the habit of greeting her daughter in the morning?

"They probably only got in a few hours ago, and I do not want to wake them," Letty murmured sleepily.

She was exhausted, undoubtedly, after he had kept her up half the night.

But panic, or at least discomfort, was rising from his gut. If he had known, he would have disappeared hours ago.

"Letty. *Letty.*"

"Hmm?" She tilted her head to look into his eyes. "What?"

He kissed the top of her head. "I have to go."

"Go?" There was immediate sadness in her tone.

He nodded. "I cannot be found here. You must see that. I need to disappear down the servants' staircase and—"

"Oh, is that how you managed to get in?" A mischievous smile appeared on her face. "I did wonder."

"Yes, and that is where I will need to disappear."

Letty tightened her grip around him, and Edward luxuriated in the feeling of her soft skin. "Not now, though."

He once again glanced at the thin sliver of light pouring through the closed curtains.

"Not immediately," he conceded, tightening his embrace. "But soon, Letty. You may be asleep when I need to go, and I will not wake you. But do not think I wish to depart."

Why did the words stick in his throat? Why did he find it impossible to understand this feeling? Emotions rushed through his body and told him she was more to him than anything.

"You will not be here when I wake up?"

It took a few minutes for Letty's breathing to return to sleep. He would give her a little more time and creep away like a thief in the night.

What had he stolen? Her innocence, perhaps, but she had stolen something from him, too, and he could not understand it. Something of his heart would be left here with Letty, and she would always have it with her.

How many young ladies had he left sleeping and spent under the bedcovers? But this was different. If he had known what this emotional connection did to him, perhaps he would have sought it earlier. He never thought he would feel this way, not after seeing how his mother had been treated by his father.

His jaw tightened. The damage that man had done to his family…

Letty had a way of making him forget all the misery.

And this obsessive desire to keep her safe, to know her better, his jealousy over anyone who spent any sort of time with her—if that were not love, what could it be?

Edward thought back to their wild passion, the unbridled exploration, the way she cried out when she experienced the height of pleasure he could give her.

There was still so much about Letty he was having to learn—announce it? Tell people that they had made love, that she had lost her innocence and therefore, her reputation?

She was far smarter than he had given her credit for.

Letty moved against him. As much as he would love to ravish her again, there was something far more appealing in curling up with her and falling asleep in each other's arms.

Edward grinned. By God, he had changed.

It was only when drifting to sleep that he realized what it was. He liked himself for more with Letty than without her.

CHAPTER ELEVEN

TRY AS SHE might, Letitia was unable to keep calm at the breakfast table.

How could she? Mere hours ago, she had been wrapped in the arms of the best gentleman she had ever met. Their skin had touched. His arms had stroked her back as she had drifted to sleep.

And before that…

Letitia shifted in her chair, hoping the salacious thoughts running through her mind could not be guessed by either of her parents. *If they could read minds, how disgusted they would be!*

Her mother looked over her teacup and frowned. Letitia hastily plastered a smile on her face and picked up her own teacup. It was cold. She had left it too long, lost in her own thoughts.

"You look…different, somehow," mused Lady Cavendish, her forehead puckering into a concerned frown.

Letitia felt the flush coming, and there was

nothing she could do to prevent it. Taking a long sip of her tea, she hoped her mother would drop the subject.

When she returned her teacup to its saucer, however, Lady Cavendish's eyes were still affixed on her.

"Different?" Letitia said, knowing she had to speak. "What do you mean?"

Unable to hold her mother's gaze, she looked down at the two fried eggs on her plate along with the sausage she had picked apart but not finished.

If only she had any sort of control over her own features—if only she could prevent her cheeks from darkening whenever she felt any amount of embarrassment!

In situations like this, when the last thing she wanted to do was speak the truth, she was immediately proven to be hiding something by her treacherous face.

"Do you not think Letitia looks different?" Lady Cavendish asked her husband.

Letitia glanced at the clock over the mantlepiece. Almost ten o'clock; far too early to leave the breakfast table without causing more questions to be asked.

Desperation to escape flooded her veins, along with irritation. *It was ridiculous she needed to ask permission to leave the table at her age—two and twenty!*

The morning's newspaper was between her and her father, who had not yet read it. In a movement of daring, she reached out, took the newspaper, and hid behind it.

It was not a cunning disguise. For one thing, she could feel the heat of her mother's glare through the paper. For another, her father was at the head of the table, and at that angle, he could still see her.

Letitia tried to concentrate on the words on the page, but it was some dull gossip about Miss Emma Tilbury—as though everyone did not know that already!—and an announcement about the Duchess of Mercia's confinement.

She could not help herself. Her eyes darted to her father.

Lord Cavendish was a tall man with a stern expression that only his nearest and dearest knew actually belied a soft and gentle temper.

He was looking at her, eyes narrowed. Letitia chanced a small smile and returned to her reading.

"No," Lord Cavendish said finally. "Letitia seems perfectly normal to me."

The tension in her shoulders melted away as she turned a page. It was rare that her father spoke out in her defense.

Not that she often needed defending. *Lord and Lady Cavendish knew their daughter well,* Letitia thought wryly. They knew attention was perhaps the thing she wished to avoid the most.

A wicked idea crossed her mind, surely any father or mother would know when their daughter had fallen in love with a gentleman who was not only the cad of the town but now engaged!

"And when are we going to announce it?"

"When the time is right, I am sure the right people will know about it."

Lady Cavendish sighed heavily. "Well, I must be wrong then."

The words were spoken with such finality that Letitia's heart started to calm, and she lowered her newspaper.

Lady Cavendish was eating a piece of toast but had not taken her eyes from her daughter. Letitia gave her a small smile.

"Anything interesting in that paper?"

Letitia folded it carefully and handed it to her father. "No, Papa. Here you go."

Lord Cavendish took the newspaper and promptly disappeared.

Letitia knew better than to catch her mother's eye again and so looked along the table for the post. Four letters had been placed on a silver platter by Bentliff, their butler, and she could see the uppermost envelope had her name on it. Picking it up, a footman immediately appeared on her right and handed her a letter opener.

"And will you be attending the Axwick ball?"

Lady Cavendish's question cut through her thoughts, and Letitia jumped, placing the letter and knife both back on the table.

"Do you not think it is strange," Letitia said in reply, "that Richard—"

"The Duke of Axwick," her mother corrected her.

Letitia blushed. "The Duke of Axwick," she said hastily, "vowed so publicly never to dance, or drink, or gamble, or marry—and now he and his wife are hosting a ball?"

"'Tis indeed a little strange," Lady Cavendish admitted, finishing off her piece of toast. "But that was not the question I asked you, Letitia. I was inquiring whether you would be attending?"

Letitia swallowed. Balls still held dread, even with the knowledge of Edward's affections.

To stand there unnoticed and unappreciated, to know she would spend the entirety of the evening wishing to dance and not being asked …

She had had nightmares about it.

"I have never been eager to attend balls, you know that," she contented herself with saying quietly, as politely as she could.

"Your interest in the matter is hardly the question here," her mother said irritably. "You are a Cavendish. It is important to be seen, Letitia, and seen at the right places. Do you think we enjoy eating that disgusting fare Lady Romeril serves up?"

Letitia smiled wearily. "No, Mama."

"No," repeated Lady Cavendish magnanimously. "And yet, do we go?"

It was like being a child again. *Was this what every young lady in their twenties experienced?* Letitia wondered.

"We do," she said quietly, knowing that was what her mother wanted to hear.

"We represent the family honor and respectability," said Lady Cavendish impressively. "And so, I ask you again. Will you be attending the Axwick ball?"

Letitia sighed and gave the only answer her mother would accept. "Of course, Mama."

As she said the words, a thought crossed her mind. *Edward, too, would surely be invited.*

Perhaps they would dance together, their first proper dance. Just the thought of being in his arms again, of receiving his attention in public, was enough to warm her.

"And will you dance?"

Her mother had been the most beautiful debutante of her Season, her father, the charming and younger Cavendish brother.

And she was the result. Plain, awkward, and unable to provoke any gentleman in society to offer her his hand for a dance.

But all that had changed.

Edward's dark eyes had brightened with desire last night when he had seen her, utterly naked. He had not recoiled or been unable to…to complete the deed.

Letitia could feel her cheeks darken again, but this ball was different. Even if Edward were not invited, she was sure a quiet request in the ear of Tabitha, the Duchess of Axwick, would be enough to see him added.

"Yes, I think I will dance," she said aloud to the visible surprise of her mother. "If…if anyone asks me. And I think they will. I…I believe Viscount Wynn will ask me to dance. He has already engaged me."

A smile crept across her face as she remembered her first meeting with him. Monty had dragged her to a pair of gentlemen, and at the time, she had not been able to think of anything worse—the Duke of Axwick, a stern man who reminded her of her father, and the gentleman she had secretly obsessed about.

How much had changed. Kisses in the carriage, kisses on the sofa, and that special kiss, which made her cry out with pleasure.

"Well, that is unexpected." Her mother's words broke into her thoughts. "Viscount Wynn, you say? Well, there will be plenty of handsome and eligible gentlemen at Axwick's ball, my girl, remember. Perhaps it is best if you forget Viscount Wynn. After all, he will have eyes for no one except Miss Lymington!"

Letitia's heart skipped a beat painfully. Her

mother's gray eyes, so like her own, were staring kindly but unwaveringly.

Did…did her mother suspect? Did she know? Was this a gentle way of attempting to warn her daughter away from the cad of the town who she believed would break her heart?

And who was Miss Lymington, and why was her mother so convinced that Edward would wish to court her?

The rush of painful emotions overwhelmed Letitia for a moment, but she finally collected herself to speak.

"Really? A-And who is Miss Lymington?"

Lady Cavendish snorted. "Oh, Letitia, I do wish you would pay attention to the gossip of society, it would save me so much time."

"You taught me not to gossip, Mama."

"I did not say you had to partake in the conversation, but listening would not do you any harm," Lady Cavendish said tartly. "That Mariah Wynn friend of yours, I suppose, has no time for gossip either. Too busy attempting to read."

"Miss Wynn has a great intellect, Mama, and if she wishes to educate herself—"

"Nonsense. No woman should seek to be so educated. Miss Wynn does herself a great disservice by seeking a university education."

Letitia waited, but no further words were forthcoming. "And?"

"She is the heiress of the Honorable Lymington and is worth thirty thousand pounds at the very least!" Lady Cavendish said with exasperation. "Viscount Wynn is a rake with no heart at all. I would not put it past him to take Miss Lymington into the card room at the Axwick ball, if they have one, of course, and win—or woo—most of her money!"

Heat blossomed across Letitia's body. She should be defending Edward. She should be saying something—but what was there to say?

Her mother's words summed up perfectly exactly what she herself had thought of him just a few weeks ago—and now they were secretly engaged to be married.

Letitia cleared her throat. "I…I do not believe he is like that."

Lady Cavendish stared in astonishment.

"Now, why do you say that, Letitia?" her mother asked. "You hardly know him."

Letitia swallowed. Perhaps, with hindsight, she should have kept her thoughts to herself.

"Over the last few weeks," she said in a voice she hoped was calm, "I have been introduced to Viscount Wynn and spoken with him on a…a number of occasions. From my conversations with him, I do not think he is that sort of gentleman."

Letitia looked nervously at her mother, who did not look convinced. "He is a distant cousin of the Duke of Axwick," she continued, a little more hastily, "and the duke has impeccable taste in companions. Viscount Wynn dined at the Devonshires' a few weeks ago, and you have known Monty and Harry their entire lives."

Poor Edward was evidently not well regarded by many. How could she feel so differently about someone her mother were so unsure of? How many other people would not consider him an appropriate guest at their table, or match for their daughter?

A seed of doubt had been planted in her heart.

Letitia bit her lip. She had heard more stories about the rakish Viscount Wynn than any other person in respectable society. Why was she suddenly so unwilling to believe them, and her own parents because of one night of pleasure?

CHAPTER TWELVE

T HE GLASS SLAMMED onto the table, and red wine slopped over the edge onto the white tablecloth.

Raucous laughter rang out around the dining room, but not loudly enough to entirely drown the groan from their host.

"Damn and blast it," Abraham Fitzclarence, Viscount Braedon, said as he threw up his hands in disgust. "You cannot control yourself for even one minute? My butler will have another word with me, and you can laugh all you like, but he is a fearsome man to behold!"

The laughter increased, and even Edward could not help but chuckle at the mock distraught on their host's face.

"No, really, I tell you I have been given notice by him, warrant you—by my own butler!" Braedon spoke with a laugh, shaking his head. "Marsh, my butler, has informed me every single one of my dinner parties ends in ruin—not for my guests, but for his linens!"

Edward laughed. By the looks of the other guests around the table, most of the red wine had flowed down gentlemen's necks rather than across the table.

The six or seven other men continued to chuckle as one of them threw out a comment about Braedon's butler being a better host, but it all washed past Edward.

Two days. It had been two days since he had last seen Letitia.

How had the earth continued to turn? Other people had continued with their busy lives, hardly caring, not knowing that the most beautiful woman in the world was out there, and not with him.

Two days. Forty-eight hours since his eyes had beheld her, since his lips had kissed her, since he had made her cry out with pleasure.

Edward tugged at his cravat, untying it in the heat of the room.

Every minute without Letitia felt hollow. As though the color had been washed out of the world.

Boredom had never been his problem, for there had always been another woman, another bed, another challenge.

"You need to get that butler in order!" Mercia spoke loudly, leaning back in his chair with a mischievous smile on his face.

He did not know the duke well, but this evening had demonstrated to him that there were far more gentlemen of worth and note in society than he had previously known.

Befriending Axwick this Season had been a wise decision. Why, if it had not been for that evening at Almack's…

"Oh, 'tis easy to blame me when finding a good butler is nigh on impossible these days!" Braedon protested. "Tell me, is there not a dearth of good servants in London at the moment?"

"I completely agree," said an older gentleman with a huge mustache. "Only last week, I had to let my valet go, and damned if I can find a replacement."

Edward stifled a yawn and glanced up at the clock. The ladies had only been gone ten minutes, and already he wished to join them.

"Servants can be so disappointing," someone else was saying. "I heard from Lord Rust…"

Reaching for his wine, Edward brought it to his lips for something to do.

Had society always been this dull? Had he simply not noticed? All this talk of servants and housekeeping.

Edward shifted in his seat and tried once again, not to yawn.

A wallflower. That had been Lady Letitia Cavendish's reputation if you had asked almost anyone in London.

But he knew better. There were so many sides of Letty, like a well-polished diamond. Every time she moved into a new setting, she sparkled.

By God, she would be able to liven them all up—if she were able to overcome her shyness.

Of all the women he could fall in love with, it was a woman who could not string three words together in the company of strangers.

Too terrified to speak, hating any notice, happy to fade into the background, none of these descriptors could be ascribed to him. They would have to learn from each other.

Letty was all he wanted to think of, and he spent another few minutes in the privacy of his own mind remembering a rather delicious moment they had shared.

"Cat got your tongue?"

Edward jumped. He had forgotten where he was, and the Duke of Axwick seemed to know it. Seated beside him, the duke was smiling.

"No, I have little to add on the topic of badly behaved servants."

Axwick raised an eyebrow. "Is that so? What secret could you share with the rest of us?"

"'Tis no secret, as far as I am aware," Edward said quietly. "I have a good butler I can depend on, and I pay my servants well. Therefore, I do not worry about them robbing me, cheating me, or leaving me."

The conversation had gone quiet. Looking up, Edward saw that all eyes in the room were staring—and Braedon had a distinct look of discomfort and even perhaps anger on his face.

"Are you saying," Braedon asked coldly, "I do not pay my servants well enough, Wynn?"

Other guests around the table were exchanging concerned glances. No one wanted a disagreement between gentlemen, especially when one was deep in liquor.

But Edward smiled. His silver tongue was enough to get him through most situations. His charm had won many an argument, helped him escape from at duels, and opened doors to ladies' bedchambers up and down the country.

Surely it would suffice here, too.

He raised his glass toward his host. "Quite the contrary, Braedon—I am saying I have had to pay my servants more, otherwise, they will leave me for you!"

The tension disappeared. The entire table roared with laughter and glasses were raised around the room to Braedon, who was now grinning with self-congratulatory pride.

"Well, I have no wish to brag," Braedon began.

"You could have fooled us!" Mercia quipped, and gentlemen banged their glasses on the table.

"That was well managed."

Edward leaned back in his chair and smiled swiftly at Axwick. "Thank you. I have had to learn how to diffuse these types of conversations, ever since my father...."

No other words were necessary, but a weight was lifted from his shoulders. The duke would not press him for more information.

"—and would you believe it," said a gentleman whom Edward did not know but was almost sure was a Mr. Kendal, "after ten minutes of speaking with her, I watched as the gentleman could still not persuade her to dance with him! Eventually, he gave her up as a bad job! It was only as a jest to tease her anyway, but he had to leave her a wallflower!"

He collapsed into laughter, and a few gentlemen joined him, but Edward could not bring himself to move or speak.

It was entirely possible this Mr. Kendal was speaking about someone other than Letty. *There must be plenty of women,* he told himself, *who did not wish to dance with Mr. Kendal and his acquaintances.*

And yet, he could not help but suspect...

"A wallflower is not a kind term," said Mercia calmly, and Edward felt gratitude to him for changing the tone of the conversation. "Nor is it kind to tease someone and pretend to wish to dance with them when one does not."

"Well, perhaps not," said the gentleman with

the huge mustache, "but sometimes it is the most accurate way to describe someone—Lady Letitia Cavendish, now!"

Edward's heart was cold, but his hands were burning. To hear her name spat out as a joke around a table was intolerable. He had to say something.

His tongue was paralyzed as more gentlemen laughed.

But Mercia's was not. "Lady Letitia Cavendish is a lovely young lady, far lovelier than many I am forced to meet, and—"

Braedon cut in. "That is all well and good, but at the same time, you cannot deny she is the epitome of a wallflower."

"I have never seen anyone want to dance with her," said another gentleman with a smirk.

It was the smirk that pushed him over the edge.

"I think you are fortunate," said Edward quietly, "that her cousin, Montague Cavendish, Duke of Devonshire, is not here to listen to you speak of his favorite cousin in such a way."

A few looked abashed, but the conversation was not over.

"Wynn, my good man," said Braedon with a hiccup, "'tis intended as no offense when one says how things are."

"I have seen the Lady Letitia dance, and dance well," Axwick said in his deep calm voice.

"I hope to see her dance again at my ball next week, at which I hope you will all join me. Mercia, are you engaged that evening?"

"I am not," said Mercia quickly, "and my wife and I are honored by your invitation. I have heard through the gossips that you have engaged St. James's court musicians. Is that true?"

Edward looked down. His hands had balled into fists, and he forced himself to release them. The conversation had moved on, thanks to Axwick and Mercia, and hopefully, it would not be too long before he could escape—or perhaps he could be bold and see if he could creep into Letty's room again.

"I do not believe it—no one would be foolish enough to actually stand up with Lady Letitia!" Mr. Kendal threw back his head to drain his glass and slammed it down to be met with silence around the table.

Edward rose to his feet. "I was."

Edward eyed Mr. Kendal.

"Oh, come on now, sir," he said jovially.

"Your jest is no longer diverting, Kendal," Braedon said quietly. "You have made your observation, now drop it."

"I only say what we are all thinking!" Mr. Kendal grinned at Edward, who felt strongly inclined to give him the same treatment as Mr. Jarvis. "Well, you are a fool then, Wynn, a fool to bother with her. Are you not interested in tupping rather than dancing? I would bet twenty guineas—no, fifty guineas that no man would wish to tup your Lady Letitia!"

Even though the table was broad, Edward lunged—and found himself held back again, this time by Axwick.

"No," Axwick murmured. "He is not worth your effort."

But Edward did not care, he wanted to hurt Mr. Kendal, make him feel the pain Letty did whenever she was abandoned at the side of a room, waiting for someone to take pity on her and take her on their arm.

God's teeth, that such a man could sit there and laugh at him, at her—at Letty! Edward's blood was boiling, and he struggled against Axwick's grip.

"Let me go," he hissed. "No man deserves to be unmarked after saying such things about—"

The sound of a heavy chair being pushed back made him stop. Braedon had risen to his feet, and there was no mirth in his face.

"Marsh," he said calmly, and the butler moved to his side. "I need your assistance."

"And I am more than willing to give it," said Marsh calmly. "Despite my ruined linens."

There was an incredible coldness in Braedon's face as he turned to face the table. "Mr. Kendal is in drink and is therefore not fit to sit at my table. Please help the gentlemen into a carriage and send a footman to see him home safely."

Mr. Kendal's mouth fell open.

He looked around the table for support, but not a single gentleman met his eye none save Edward, who glared, pulse racing, heart thundering in his chest.

"Fine," spat Mr. Kendal, throwing down his napkin and rising to his feet.

A pair of footmen appeared, marching him out of the room. The butler closed the door behind them, but the tension remained.

"Thank you," Edward said curtly to his host.

Braedon nodded briefly, and the two gentlemen sat down.

There was a moment of silence, broken by the mustached gentleman.

"Well, I think it is time for me to call it a night," he said awkwardly, rising to his feet. "Thank you for your hospitality, Viscount Braedon, it is much appreciated. I am sure my wife and I would be pleased to host you ourselves in the coming weeks."

A few other gentlemen gratefully took this as their time to depart, and within minutes, Edward was left at the table with his host, Mercia, and Axwick.

Mercia cleared his throat. "Wynn, I have no wish to offend you, and I have a great regard for Lady Letitia—but I do not understand your pointed defense of her."

Edward gripped the arms of his chair, trying to control his temper. *Why could no one leave her alone?* No wonder she felt so uncomfortable being introduced to him.

"I have a...a regard for Lady Letitia," he said stiffly. "And I do not like gossip, particularly when it is cruel."

"I think we would agree with you on those latter two points," Mercia said mildly. "But I am intrigued to better understand your regard for her. If you think to wed her, I urge you to reconsider. Her father would never permit a union between you."

Edward's temper had only just begun to recede, and the slight insult was enough to prick it once more. "How dare you—why would he never permit such a thing? Not that...if I was interested, I mean."

Curse it, why could he not hide his emotions when it came to Letty? In every other quarter of his life, he could control himself.

Beside him, Axwick was laughing. "Wynn, she is a Cavendish! They are an incredibly wealthy family, full of pride and self-importance. Monty is different, of course, but his uncle, Letitia's father, is far too aware of his own worth."

Edward swallowed. He had not known much about the Cavendish family; they were far too well-bred to associate with the Wynns when he had been young.

"Well, she is the junior branch," he said awkwardly, suddenly aware that he was alone in a room with two dukes and a more senior viscount. "At least, that is my understanding."

Braedon sighed. "Yes, but you would not know that by the way her father acts. He seems utterly convinced the line should have gone to him and not to Devonshire. Mark my words, no one but an earl will be good enough for little Letitia."

Edward sat in stunned silence.

Axwick appeared to sense his discomfort. "Well, I can understand his concern. My little one is but a few months old, and I have already received two letters from mamas of little girls seeking an alliance!"

Braedon guffawed, and Mercia's eyes widened. "No, surely not!"

"On my honor!" Axwick chuckled. "I know it is strange, but my Tabitha actually took it as a great compliment, although God knows how to respond to such letters. My mother once said…"

Edward's mind was utterly overwhelmed with his companions' words.

He had not seriously considered marrying Letty; he had not considered marrying anyone.

But to be told in such an abrupt fashion that he would not stand a chance in convincing Letty's father, he suddenly found himself wanting to impress him, wanting to be good enough.

It was childish, and it was contrary, but that was the sort of man he was.

Why was Letitia such a bewitching woman, such a puzzle and a challenge, even when she was not trying to be?

CHAPTER THIRTEEN

S MOOTHING DOWN HER gown did not work, nor did closing her eyes and breathing slowly.

Letitia opened her eyes and swallowed. Panic fluttered in her stomach, making it almost impossible to stand still. Her hands were shaking.

Why was it like this every time? She should be accustomed to it, but every time she was about to walk into a room of strangers, she was overwhelmed.

She looked up at the night sky. Stars were visible through the clouds and smog. It must be almost eight o'clock, and the invitation for Miss Ashbrooke's card party had indicated seven.

Laughter poured out of the open front door. Its abruptness made Letitia jump and pull her pelisse around her more tightly.

You are being ridiculous, she told herself. *You probably know half the people in that card party, and as it is, there will be no dancing. Smile and chatter with them for a few hours.*

Lying to herself had never been that easy, and even the hope Edward may be inside was not enough to take those last few steps to the doorway.

Edward. He had not been far from her mind since their last meeting three days ago. *Why had he stayed away?*

The thought was painful, and Letitia pushed it away.

But despite her desperation, Letitia was too terrified to move forward, too absorbed in her own hopes and fears to move back.

If Edward were there, what would he say to her? What emotions would be stirred in her own heart when she saw her betrothed across a crowded room?

How will they manage to speak without revealing their passion and devotion?

Letitia smiled. Or even worse, what if Edward were not in there, what if he had not been invited?

How was she to endure another evening without him?

"Careful, miss!"

Letitia gasped as someone brushed past her as they entered Miss Ashbrooke's card party. The gentleman glanced back at her, and she felt her cheeks flush.

Was she always to be ignored save for a

curious glance?

The gentleman squinted, struggling to see her in the gloom of the evening, and Letitia turned her head.

When she turned back to look into the bright glare of the open doorway, he was gone.

She sighed, watching her breath blossom into the night. This was madness, and if she could not summon up the courage to walk into a card party alone, she should go home.

Her fingers tightened on her invitation. She was *not* going to be a wallflower for the rest of her life.

Swallowing painfully, she stepped forward and walked through the door to see a footman waiting for her invitation.

"My lady," he murmured with a bow and gestured that she was to enter.

It took only ten seconds to see her hopes for a quiet card party would be disappointed. Miss Ashbrooke had promised her an intimate evening with a few close friends. A loud cheer went up in a room to her left as the door opened, and a billowing cloud of cigar smoke blossomed out in the hallway.

Letitia coughed, waving her hand before her to dispel the smoke from her stinging eyes and bumped into a gentleman.

"Watch out there!" he said roughly, shoving her back, so she almost lost her footing.

"I-I do apologize," Letitia stammered. Now the smoke had cleared, she could see the hallway was as packed as the card rooms seemed to be. Ladies promenaded up and down as though at Brighton taking the waters, with gentlemen admiring them.

Stumbling down the corridor, another door was open, but shouting cheers echoed out of it, and she wandered to an opposite door, which she wrenched open.

Music blasted her ears, and there was hysterical laughter and the sound of a glass smashing on the floor.

Letitia stepped back into the corridor and leaned against the wall, trying to fight down nausea.

This was not what she wanted at all. Music would mean there was dancing. She did not want to be left out again. Could she not attend one party this Season without the pressure of being forced to dance?

"What are you doing here, then?" A gentleman she did not recognize leered. "Not lost, are you my sweet? I am sure I can find you a home if you want one."

Letitia shrank away but could not escape the disgusting fumes of liquor pouring from the gentleman.

"N-No," she managed, "I am quite well, thank you, I-I do not need—"

"You look like you could do with a friend." He grinned, and Letitia's stomach dropped. "I could be your friend."

Unable to think what to say, she glanced back into the room with the dancing—and saw a flash of almost midnight black hair.

Edward.

Without saying another word, she darted into the room.

Someone waved from the corner—it was Mariah, seated as always with a book in her lap.

But Letitia wanted Edward. No one else had hair in that precise shade. Her eyes darted around the room, desperate to find him.

There were four couples dancing in a square, and one of them stared in confusion.

"Lost, child?" one of them shouted.

But Letitia was not lost.

Without heeding the shout or any of the curious gazes now following her, she stepped across the room toward the tall gentleman with dark brown eyes who was a beacon of safety in the wilderness of the party.

"Ed—Viscount Wynn!"

She had not intended to speak his name aloud. And she knew people were watching—even wallflowers had to protect their reputations.

But as his eyes lifted and met hers, Letitia's spirits rose immediately. How was it possible that he cared for her? Of all the young ladies he had met this Season, it had been *she* with whom he had fallen in love.

Well. Perhaps he had not spoken those words exactly, but he had made love to her, and told her so—told her that it was different somehow.

"I have bedded other women. I have not made love to them. I want to make love to you."

If that was not proof of his affection, what was? And because he had taken her innocence, were they not betrothed? Hadn't he suggested it?

She reacted instinctively. He was smiling a little woodenly when she reached out and took his hands in hers.

She could not help but smile. "Shall we stand up for the next dance?"

His hands were so warm and strong. She felt safer now than she ever had.

There was a polite cough, but it did not come from Edward. Letitia glanced to her left to see a beautiful young woman standing between her and Edward—a woman who had evidently been standing there the entire time, but Letitia obliviously ignored.

Letitia blinked. The woman was her age, perhaps a little younger, with carefully curled ringlets falling around her eyes and a slightly incredulous smile on her face.

Heat rushed to Letitia's cheeks. She had evidently interrupted what was a private conversation, and if the woman's features were any indication, Letitia was not welcome.

"Well," breathed the young lady with a laugh, "I do not believe we have met."

Letitia opened her mouth to speak, but no words came out. Furious with herself, she tried to conjure up something, anything.

"I…uh…"

The woman glanced at Edward and smiled coquettishly. "Why, Wynn, in all our conversations, you never mentioned you had another lady friend in town. Why do you not introduce me to your…acquaintance?"

What had she thought she was doing, asking a gentleman to dance—and in public!

Letitia's gaze darted to Edward, who was evidently uncomfortable, too. He shifted on his feet, looking between the two young ladies.

The young lady was still smiling at Edward as though she had him hypnotized, and Letitia tried not to notice her confidence and beauty.

"She is the heiress of the Honorable Lymington and is worth thirty thousand pounds at the very least! Viscount Wynn is a rake with no heart at all. I would not put it past him to take Miss Lymington into the card room at the Axwick ball if they have one, of course, and win—or woo—most of her money!"

Were her parents correct? Was Edward no longer interested in her, perhaps never had been, and would continue on with his rakish ways?

Would he ignore her now, shun her in public?

How could she have been so stupid to give her innocence to him?

Edward coughed. "Lady Letitia Cavendish," he said awkwardly, "may I introduce you to the Lady Antoinette d'Michel."

Letitia bobbed a quick curtsey.

"Lady Antoinette d'Michel, Lady Letitia Cavendish," Edward said quietly. "Lady Antoinette is my cousin, Lady Letitia, and moved to England after the troubles in France a few years ago. She arrived in London yesterday, and Miss Ashbrooke was kind enough to include her in my invitation."

Letitia swallowed. This was the moment when she had to speak. *Speak!*

"I am honored to make your acquaintance, Lady Antoinette," she managed. "And I am glad to hear you have found entertainment in town with…with your cousin."

Cousin, she thought ruefully. If she had been but a sister, another adopted sister perhaps—but cousin. They wed all the time.

And she was handsome, prodigiously so. Lady Antoinette outshone the rest of the room. Even now, Letitia could feel the gazes of many other gentlemen in the room, moving to the French beauty.

None were looking at her.

She had not come over here to be belittled

and shamed; she had asked Edward to dance—but now she thought of it, he had not answered.

"Yes, it is truly wonderful to be taken in by one's family—our mothers were sisters, you know," Lady Antoinette said playfully, placing her hand on Edward's arm. Letitia could not pretend she hadn't seen it, her heart growing cold. "We had not seen each other for so many years, and when my poor Papa—"

"I do not think Lady Letitia wants to hear the details," Edward interrupted. "I am sure it is not a topic you yourself wish to dwell on, either."

"Perhaps you would like to dance," Letitia said timidly, not knowing why she was so bold, but knowing she would regret it forever if she did not. "I have heard, Viscount Wynn, that you enjoy dancing."

Letitia's heart was in her mouth as she waited for his response.

Edward glanced around him. Gentlemen were listening to the conversation—whether because Lady Antoinette was such a beauty, or because Letitia had shamed herself, she could not tell.

It was like being locked in a cage, and Letitia stared. *Why did he just not say yes?*

"I...I would—of course, yes," Edward said finally.

But his gaze dropped, and Letitia saw, with horror, something akin to shame on his features.

He was ashamed of her. Of course he was; she should have known his attentions to her would always be in private, not public.

"I do not wish to be a burden or a chore," she said quietly. "If you do not wish to dance, all you need say is—"

"I do," Edward interrupted, still not looking at her. "But, I know I cannot expect you to leave off being a wallflower for my sake."

Letitia stared. She had wanted to see him, hear his voice, be close to him.

But this was not the Edward she knew. Did he call her a wallflower? After all he had said to her before, after all his bluster about replanting her?

He had called her a wallflower, in public, and before a woman who looked as though she was stifling down her laughter with great difficulty.

She was a Cavendish. She would not allow her emotions to run away with her. She would keep them in check.

"I thought that was precisely what I was doing. I had thought," she said as coldly as she could muster, "I was leaving my wallflower days behind me. I was mistaken."

Turning away, she tried to keep her watering eyes from Lady Antoinette's view.

She reached the hallway corridor when someone took her hand. Letitia turned to see Edward, an emotion she did not recognize burning in his eyes.

"Follow me."

A thousand thoughts rushed through her mind. Why should she trust him now? Why had he brought this Lady Antoinette to Miss Ashbrooke's, to flaunt her? Why had he not jumped at the chance to dance with her, and had instead left her to the merciless wit of society?

But none of those emotions formed into conscious sentences. Edward, his hand still enclosed over hers, pulled her down the corridor. They rushed past bowing footmen and curious guests until they reached a door that Edward threw open.

Letitia gasped as the freezing cold air of the night hit her face. It was the door into the garden, and they stepped into the night.

Only then did Edward let go of her hand. He stopped dead and turned to look at her.

Letitia wrapped her arms around herself, trying not to shiver. His face was illuminated by the light cascading through the windows.

Edward smiled faintly. "You took me by surprise."

Trying to take a deep breath, Letitia examined his features. He did look genuinely wretched and more than a little conflicted.

"I had no wish to force you to do anything," she said quietly. "You were perfectly at liberty to do whatever you wanted, Edward. I am… I am not your keeper, at least not publicly. But how can I trust you, how can you think I will trust you if you act—"

"I did not expect—I did not expect you to be here at all, to be frank," Edward said softly and took a step toward her, but she stepped back. "You…you have never been so direct with me before, Letty. I hardly knew what to do with myself."

"I find that hard to believe! You are in society daily. You do not think that a woman could be bold?"

Her words were fierce, far more determined than she felt. Just looking at him melted all her anger, but underneath was pain, and that did not disappear. How could he have just stood there?

Edward looked just as confused at his own behavior. "I have no words, my darling. Have you never been thrown in a conversation, lost in the moment, unsure how to act?"

Of course she had; that was her life. It was difficult to believe that this confident, rakish man felt the same. "You are not accustomed to a strong woman?"

Edward chuckled and shook his head. "No, 'tis not that. I am not accustomed to you being a strong woman, Letty, but I like it."

He took another step closer, and this time, Letitia did not step away. Having him so close to her but not touching was sweet torture. All she could think about was the last time his hands had touched her, what pleasure he had given her—they had given each other.

"I also liked the wallflower," he whispered. "I missed her, Letty."

Edward leaned forward to kiss her, and she responded with complete abandon.

"I missed you," she managed to gasp between wild kisses. "Edward…"

"God, Letty, I wanted to kiss you the moment you walked into that room," he moaned.

Their passion overtook them. Letitia gave no thought to who could be watching them through the windows; this was Edward, his hands in her hair, his lips crushed on hers.

His hand grazed her breasts, and she hated the clothes keeping his touch from her. Every part of her seemed to awake in his presence like nothing else. The thought he could have already ceased to care for her and was more interested in that woman—but she had believed it so quickly.

Who would be interested in Letitia the wallflower?

Eventually, their kisses tailed off, but she remained in his arms.

"I do not like keeping this, us, a secret," she whispered.

Edward grinned. "I think 'tis the most enjoyable thing about it."

She could not help herself. She laughed, and

Edward kissed her forehead as she leaned against his chest.

"That is all very well," she said quietly, "but you are the rake, not I. When are we going to—"

"We should go back inside, you will catch your death of cold," Edward interrupted, lifting her chin up, so she looked into his eyes. "And I would never forgive myself if you were to become unwell because of my selfishness."

"What about your cousin?"

"She is here for an extended visit, and perhaps the two of you will become friends."

Letitia nodded, but something uncomfortable remained at the back of her mind. He was more open in society with his cousin than he was with her. Was this to be her courtship with Edward, then, in secret, so no one else could know?

Was he being entirely honest with her? Was he really thrown by her boldness, or was Viscount Wynn, the society rake, ashamed of her?

CHAPTER FOURTEEN

EDWARD CRANED HIS neck painfully. "I cannot see her."

Abraham Fitzclarence, Viscount Braedon, sighed and shook his head. "Of course not, you dolt—you are looking in entirely the wrong direction!"

Edward ceased looking around the crush of the Axwick ball and punched Braedon lightly on the shoulder.

"You are the one who is supposed to be telling me where to look!"

"I have only seen her once before!" Braedon protested with a mock wince, rubbing where Edward's fist had landed. "God's teeth, man, how am I supposed to find anyone in this crush? Axwick invited the entirety of London, by the look of it."

"I am surprised to see so many people," Edward agreed, smoothing his cravat as his eyes darted around the crowd. "I thought the intention was a small and intimate party?"

Braedon scoffed as they stepped aside to stop from being flattened by a gaggle of young ladies, all giggling and wearing so many feathers, birds seemed to fly through the air.

"Axwick is such a light touch. Five or six people probably requested additional invitations, and each of them brought a guest..." Braedon raised his eyebrows. "You know Axwick."

Edward nodded. He had heard the mysterious Miss Lymington would be here, and he had been curious to see her for a while. When he met with Braedon within minutes of arriving at the ball, he had promised he could point her out—but so far, he had been utterly useless.

"If you exaggerated meeting her before, Braedon, just say now," he said easily. "I will hold no grudge against you, I want the truth."

Braedon's eyes widened in jesting horror. "To think that you would doubt my word, my honor, even, because I cannot espy one woman in a crowd of hundreds! Give me but a moment, and I will find her for you. Ladies do not come by order, you know!"

Edward laughed as he helped himself to a glass of red wine.

Well, at least the Axwick ball would be bearable with Braedon by his side. He was a character, and as a viscount himself, there was a natural comfort between the two gentlemen. Neither was too impressed by the other, neither felt the awkwardness of imbalanced nobility.

Braedon was still glancing around the room like a startled puppy, and Edward had to stifle a laugh. He had not been entirely sure whether he had liked Braedon at first and had only accepted his invitation to dine because Braedon was well connected.

That had all changed when Braedon had thrown that disgraceful Kendal from his house. His quick thinking and demonstrable honor had proven that, while Braedon still had a few rough edges, there was some gold in him somewhere.

"There—see her?"

Braedon interrupted his thoughts and nudged his shoulder. Edward glanced up.

About twenty feet away and surrounded by admirers was a woman with black hair, shining eyes, and confidence few women ever had.

"That is Miss Lymington, heiress of the *ton*," Braedon muttered. "None are her equal. She has more than thirty thousand pounds, no family to speak of, and is apparently open to suggestions."

Edward laughed. "I know what open to suggestions means, I am no fool born yesterday. She has someone in mind but will not say."

She did seem remarkably self-assured, even for a lady who was worth more than most of the other young ladies at the ball combined. There was something intriguing about Miss Lymington, something intoxicating. Edward could feel it, even from here.

She was a natural charmer, and it took one to know one. Edward watched as she carefully paid enough attention to the gentlemen closest to her, but gave delicious glances to the gentlemen outside of her immediate circle.

Edward shook his head with a smile. *A remarkable woman.*

Braedon drained his drink and smacked his lips. "Well, you are the expert in this area, Wynn, so I bow to your superior knowledge—but no one has made an offer. 'Tis hard to know whether anyone will be good enough for her."

Miss Lymington laughed, and at least three gentlemen preened on the assumption it had been their words which had made her smile.

Edward grinned knowingly. God, he had used similar tricks himself, and it had made ladies simply throw themselves at him. He was not looking at a natural; he was looking at a professional.

"Will you try for her?"

Edward hesitated before speaking.

His instinct was no. Miss Lymington could not consider him, and he would be a fool to try and convince himself of anything different.

The lady had thirty thousand pounds. More. That put her in the highest leagues, more wealthy than even someone with the pedigree of Lady Letitia Cavendish. Anyone with that size inheritance would not be looking for a viscount; she would be angling for a title far more impressive—a duke maybe. Where better to meet eligible gentlemen than at a duke's ball?

Watching Miss Lymington walk sedately around the room, happy in the knowledge that she was by far the wealthiest woman in the room, made Edward think a little more deeply.

His heart belonged to Letty, even if he would not admit it. But the habits of a lifetime were hard to break. What a fantastic challenge to see if he could make Miss Lymington fall in love with him.

He had no wish to harm her, no wish to break her heart—but what a test of his charms.

No, he was not seriously considering Miss Lymington as the future Viscountess Wynn.

But wouldn't it be interesting to see?

"Ah, I thought as much."

Edward jumped to see Braedon with a knowing smile on his face.

"Thought what?"

"Christ alive, man, I was not born yesterday, although I may act like it," said Braedon breezily. "I can see you have decided to go after her."

Edward swallowed. *Was he that transparent?* "I have made no such decision."

The glass in his hand felt heavy. If Braedon, a

gentleman he hardly knew, had seen his decision, how would he ever keep anything from Miss Lymington—or Letty?

"Why not?" Braedon shrugged, waving his empty glass at a footman who immediately bobbed his head and disappeared. "You are not engaged to be married, and the more I know you, Wynn, the more I am convinced you never will be."

Just a few months ago, he would agree with his new friend; but without any warning, a vision of Letitia walking down the aisle to him in the most beautiful and yet simple gown, with a veil over her eyes, flashed into his mind.

Something lurched in his stomach. It would not be the end of the world if he found himself married to Letty. A lifetime of laughter with her? Hidden away in Redmont, where no one could ever bother them, and they could simply enjoy each other's company—and each other's bodies?

It was certainly not a terrible future.

"Ah, there's Lady Letitia Cavendish."

Edward almost cricked his neck. Braedon was right. Letty had entered the room on the arm of the Duchess of Devonshire, looking a little overwhelmed at the crush.

Relief spread through his body. Letty was with Harry, and although it still made him feel a little discomforted to refer to one of the most noble woman in the country with such a nickname, at least she was with a friend.

"Oh, look," Braedon said nonchalantly. "She is waving at you."

"Miss Lymington?" Edward turned to see where the woman had wandered.

Braedon laughed. "No, not Miss Lymington, you dolt, she does not know you from Adam. No, Lady Letitia. I must say, Wynn, you evidently know her far better than you let on at my dining table."

Edward saw Letty waving at him, and his stomach twisted.

"She is…we are acquainted," he managed.

God, but she was beautiful. Even in a crowd, not a single person compared to Letitia Cavendish. How did no one else see it? His heart twisted painfully at the competing desires: to speak with Letty, maybe even dance with her—or to finally speak to Miss Lymington?

He had seen the Earl of Marnmouth earlier, and an earldom was a far more impressive title than viscount. Was he already speaking with Miss Lymington?

If he did not decide soon, he would lose all opportunity to speak with the wealthy heiress. He would be last in the queue to speak with her, and all opportunity to test himself would be gone.

Edward bowed his head to Letty and turned to Braedon.

"Wish me luck," he muttered as he handed his half-empty glass to his companion.

Braedon broke out into a grin. "God's teeth, but you are braver than I. Good luck, sir!"

Even weaving between the slightly inebriated older gentlemen and the ladies clucking to encourage their daughters into the paths of the right gentlemen, Edward did not lose sight of Miss Lymington.

She was standing with five or six gentlemen, each hanging on her every word.

"You know, you look nothing like what I had been told," Edward said grandly as he arrived at the gathering.

The Earl of Marnmouth glared.

But Miss Lymington did not. Edward was unsure whether it was the rude lack of introduction or his boldness. He knew his charm was usually enough to get a woman's attention, but this situation was different.

Miss Lymington raised an eyebrow. "Why, Viscount Wynn, you flatter me...I think."

Edward grinned, allowing his head to tilt. "Well, that is the question, is it not. You know me, which is impressive. Now I am the one who is flattered."

"Wynn, I was just saying," began Marnmouth, but he was interrupted.

"Now then, Marnmouth, let the poor man speak," Miss Lymington said with a smile. She stepped toward Edward and tapped him on the chest with her fan. "I know every eligible gentleman who is here. I have made it my business to know."

"Oh, and why is that?" Edward spoke lightly, but his entire body felt as though it was on fire. *God, this was it; the heady to and fro, the delicate words carefully chosen, the ability to drive desire in a woman before he had even touched her.*

It was a gift. It was why he had been such a successful rake. If he could rile up a lady before he had even pushed up her skirts and showed her what real pleasure was—

"Because you all know who I am," said Miss Lymington, "and I would hate to be on the back foot, especially when there are so many of you and only one of me."

She smiled through her lashes and fluttered her fan. My word, if he was the master of seduction, she was its mistress. They could drive each other wild, but this moment was more than enough for him.

Edward frowned, carefully allowing it to grow naturally. "Know you? Why should everyone know you, Miss Jones? I must apologize, Marnmouth, I have interrupted you. Please do continue."

Miss Lymington's mouth opened, but before she could say a word, Edward bowed and turned on his heels.

He walked away slowly and tried to keep his face neutral. One, two, three…

"Excuse me!"

Someone tapped him on the shoulder, and Edward turned to see Miss Lymington, a picture of anger, had followed him and left her gaggle of gentlemen behind.

"You are excused?" he said in a confused voice.

"I am not a Miss Jones!" Miss Lymington looked outraged and did not concern herself with keeping her voice down. Faces turned to stare, and if she had thought it would cause him to shrink back, she was wrong.

Edward grinned. This was the place he belonged, front and center with a beautiful woman before him.

"My word, I am sorry, you must accept my apologies," he said with a shrug. "I was certain you were…you are not Miss Jones?"

Miss Lymington's mouth fell open. "You are in earnest."

"Never more so," lied Edward happily. *God, this made him feel alive.* "And you are…?"

"You…you do not know who I am?" Miss Lymington said in horror.

Edward looked her up and down, and muffled giggles emerged from the crowd gathered around them.

"My dear lady," he said slowly, raising his

voice to ensure the crowd would hear him, "although you are a very pretty young thing, there are plenty of pretty young things in London. I cannot be expected to know the names of you all."

Raucous laughter erupted around the room. Edward did his best not to grin, but it was almost too much. He could not remember the last time he had had so much fun—God, it must have been what, that card party at the beginning of the Season?

"Wynn, you dog!"

"Give him a slap!"

True, his cousin Axwick would hardly want his ball to become a public nuisance, but surely it was worth it to see such horror and shock on Miss Lymington's face.

It was time to take this woman down a peg or two. She had clearly enjoyed her own importance, and as he had no interest in bedding or wedding her, it would be a public service to whoever was hooked by her wealth and beauty next.

"I am Miss Lymington," she said, utterly incensed, "and I have some thirty thousand pounds, that is why you should know who I am!"

Edward gasped and shook his head seriously, taking a step toward her. "Miss Lymington, shame on you! 'Tis very bad manners to be announcing one's fortune to a crowd!"

Before he allowed her to get a word into the conversation, Edward took another step toward her so that he could whisper into her ear.

"And if you are not careful, Miss Lymington," he murmured, his breath tickling her neck, "I shall have to teach you a lesson."

Miss Lymington stared, her cheeks still crimson, but her demeanor changed.

"Why, my lord," she said with a smile far more flirtatious than anything she had given to Marnmouth or any of the other gentlemen fawning over her minutes ago. "Will you indeed? I am not sure whether I am a quick learner."

Edward grinned. By God, he had been right; she was the closest thing a woman could be to a rake. If he did not have the presence of mind and a heart belonging to Letty, he would probably be in danger.

"Then I will have to dedicate a serious amount of time to your study," Edward said quietly without taking his eyes from her. "And I will have to punish you if necessary."

Scandalized gasps erupted around them, and Edward winked again before glancing at the crowd of people who had moved around them. Why should he not? He was breaking no rules, had made no promises, and by the looks of it, had only upset gentlemen too dull to catch Miss Lymington's eye.

His face froze. There, standing a foot behind

Miss Lymington and with a look of horror on her face, close enough to catch every single word he had said, was Letty.

"My word, sir," Miss Lymington said with a giggle, hitting him once again with her fan, "you are truly the most—sir?"

But Edward was not listening. His focus was on Letty, who had disappeared into the crowd.

"Letitia!"

Miss Lymington looked behind her curiously as the crowd stared.

Letty had not stopped. She was now almost beyond his line of sight, the crush of Axwick's guests swallowing her up.

Could she not hear him? Edward felt panic rise in his throat as he pushed unceremoniously past Miss Lymington and stepped in Letty's direction.

It was a flirtatious jest, an innocent test of his charm and prowess—but in God's name, he had never intended Letty to hear it. He had not wanted her to, and it was only now the horror in her eyes was seared across his own that he realized why.

Damn his conscience, which had given him no warning. Damn his pride, which had wanted the confirmation that he still had the ability to make a woman go weak in the knees.

"Wynn?"

Braedon's voice could be heard through the

crowd, but Edward did not heed him.

"Letitia!"

Either she did not hear him, or she did not want to. Edward could not fight through the crowd quickly enough. Forcing himself into the hallway, he finally snapped.

"Out of my way!"

Lady Romeril glared. "Well, that is no way to speak to—"

"Move!" Edward did not care if he offended half of society. It was Letitia who mattered to him, and if he was not wrong, he had made a terrible mistake.

CHAPTER FIFTEEN

U PROAR SURROUNDED HER, but Letitia could not hear it. People's mouths were opening, but no sound reached her ears.

All she could hear was her own anger.

How—how could he do that?

No, she must not think. Letitia pushed past another gentleman in her way. The door to the hallway was getting further away the more she pushed toward it.

"Letitia—Letitia, what is wrong?" Harry's voice cried, but Letitia could not stop and explain.

How could she explain when she did not understand it herself? Edward, her Edward, had said those things—such things…

No, she had to escape here before the tears fell. She had never cried in public before, and she would not start now.

She was a Cavendish. Cavendishes did not fall apart in public. They did it in private.

"Letitia!"

That voice was different, and through the blurred mirage of the crowd, Letitia could make out Mariah Wynn trying to push her way toward her, with spectacles still on her nose.

But Letitia did not want to speak with anyone. How would she even begin to articulate the betrayal in her heart, when the person who had committed the crime was a gentleman she barely knew?

"And if you are not careful, Miss Lymington, I shall have to teach you a lesson."

Letitia hardened her heart. She had to leave this place.

"Letitia!"

It was Edward's voice, but she did not allow herself to turn around. *Let him shout after her, let him feel even a portion of the pain she was feeling right now.* He had said those words to a woman he had evidently just met.

And she had been standing right there. How had he not seen her? How many other women had he spoken to like that? How many since she had handed over to him the most vulnerable part of her? When she had lost her innocence, and perhaps her reputation to him?

The hallway was even busier, the front door open, welcoming new guests.

Only another few feet, and she would be free of this cloying sensation that everyone was staring.

"My word, Lady Letitia!" A woman was walking towards her, and people melted out of her way—the hostess of the evening, Tabitha St. Maur, the Duchess of Axwick. "You look flushed, are you unwell?"

"I wish to go home," she said. "Please call me a carriage, Your Grace."

Tabitha looked at her closely but did not ask any questions. Glancing up, a footman melted out of the crowd and to her side.

"A carriage for my friend, Lady Letitia Cavendish," Tabitha said swiftly. "As quickly as you can. She needs to go home immediately."

The footman bowed, and Letitia felt a rush of gratitude to the woman who barely knew her.

"Th-Thank you," she managed.

Tabitha squeezed her hand. "You are not the first, and you will not be the last. I hope the rest of your evening is restful, my lady."

And with that, the hostess was gone.

"Letitia!"

She did not look back. She knew it was Edward. She would wait for the carriage and damn those who stared. *Let them stare.* She had done nothing wrong—and she was Lady Letitia Cavendish, after all.

"Letitia, wait!"

But she would not wait. What could he possibly have to say to her that could explain away his behavior?

All she wanted to do was escape this terrible place and hide.

"My lady," bowed the footman as she reached the front door.

"Her Grace has ordered me a carriage," said Letitia a little breathlessly. "May I wait here with you until—oh!"

A hand grabbed her arm. Edward had finally caught up with her.

"Letty, I—"

"Let go of me!" She wrenched her arm from his grip, and to the horror of the footman, ran down the steps and into the night.

"Letty, I am sorry!"

Letitia turned to face him. Edward stepped back.

"You do not even know what you are apologizing for, so I would rather you stopped," she said curtly. To her surprise, the instinct to cry had disappeared, and all that was left was anger. "How—how dare you treat me in that way! How dare you do it in front of me! Do you have no honor, sir?"

Part of her wanted to hear his defense, to hear some sort of excuse that would wash away the sin of what he had done—but it was a small part of her.

"I know my own way home, I have no need of a carriage," she said abruptly. "Good evening,

Viscount Wynn."

She started striding down the street.

She should have known it simply would not work. Within a heartbeat, Edward was walking alongside her.

"It was merely a jest, Letty—"

"That is not what it looked like from where I was standing, your lordship," Letitia said sharply, not taking her eyes from the pavement. "And it did not look like that to the Duke of Axwick's guests, if I am any judge. Or Miss Lymington."

It was an effort to keep bitterness from her tone, but Letitia had the right. They had not formally announced anything, no one was to know what they were to each other, so she should not feel hatred towards Miss Lymington.

But Edward? He knew exactly how she felt about him, how could he not? She had allowed him…they had shared something so special, so precious.

Did he think she was happy to walk away from him, that it did not break her heart?

Edward pulled on her arm. "It was a flirtation, Letty, that was all."

"I am not a total fool," she snapped. *Did he think her a complete innocent?* "I did not expect it to be so blatant, so disgusting, and worst of all, with another woman!"

It felt good to say these things, to almost shout them. Was this what it felt like to be everyone else? Unafraid to say how you really felt, feeling joy in speaking your mind?

"I have spent my entire life attempting to blend in, hide in the background, be unnoticed by the world," she said fiercely, pulling her arm from his grip and turning left onto another dark, quiet street. "I never thought that one day that skill would betray me. You did not even see me, Edward. You did not see me! Do not pretend that you did, for I shall be most offended, and—"

"Letty, stop!" Edward finally managed to slow her to a halt. "You are upset, and I completely understand why, but we need to talk about it properly. Were you honestly going to walk all the way home? In the dark? Alone?"

The last word seemed to echo. Letitia stared into Edward's dark eyes, trying desperately not to allow her anger to disappear. She had to use it as a tool. As a weapon. Perhaps she would hurt him as he had hurt her.

"I did not think I was alone," she said finally. "Perhaps I am."

Edward dropped his gaze. "God's teeth, Letty, the way you look at me...as though I am nothing, as though I am scum."

Letitia did not respond. He needed to feel this. If it was a pinch of what she felt, it was worth it. She loved him so much, and it was a wildly complicated feeling—the desire to be crushed into his arms, to be held by him, but also to make him feel the pain that was raging in her body and soul.

"Look, I am not proud of it, but that…that way of speaking to women…" Edward looked at her with desperation. "Letitia, that has been a huge part of who I am for years—over a decade! Being a cad, flirting, jesting with a beautiful woman, it is not something one can simply switch off!"

"I have changed for you," Letitia said simply. Most of the anger had gone from her voice, but pain was still there. "I was a wallflower, too terrified to think of even speaking to a gentleman, and I changed for you."

Edward opened his mouth but then closed it again. There was a look of utter wretchedness on his face.

She stepped forward. "I gave myself to you, Edward. I opened myself up to you, body and soul. I-I risked my reputation, lost my innocence. And you do not think it worth trying a little harder to stop flirting with other women?"

"'Tis not as simple as that."

"It is," Letitia said simply. "And if you cannot see that…"

She did not want to say it. There was a carriage waiting outside the Axwicks'. Letitia turned to retrace her steps, and it was not until she had turned the corner back onto Axwick's street that he appeared at her side again.

"You do not understand—I have a reputation to uphold."

Letitia laughed bitterly. "I have risked my reputation for you, and on the promise that when I allowed you to bed me, it was more than that. It was because you loved me, and now I am starting to wonder, was that a lie?"

Letitia did what she promised she would not do; she looked at him.

Was this the moment he admitted he was in love with her, and only her?

"I...I never actually said that I loved you, Letty, but—no, wait!"

His words cut her more deeply than she thought possible.

"How can you..." Letitia did not even know how to finish that sentence.

They had reached the Axwick residence, and a footman had run down the steps to meet her.

"Your carriage is almost ready, my lady."

Letitia nodded, and the servant disappeared with obvious relief.

"You are running away."

Edward's voice was laced with disappointment, but Letitia laughed bitterly.

"Yes, from you."

"No, I meant from how you feel."

The sounds of a ball at its height poured from the open door. If only she could be in there, standing by the dancers like the wallflower she was, with Mariah by her side.

"You have no idea how I feel, and if you did, or you cared about me in any way, you would not have spoken that way to Miss Lymington," said Letitia quietly. "What if she thinks you care, that you have serious intentions for her?"

Edward laughed, and Letitia's heart squeezed painfully. He was so handsome, so unbearably charming. "Oh, Letty, she would have to be an idiot to think that."

"Like I was? Like I was an idiot to think that you would care for me?"

"What—no!" Edward swore under his breath. "I—Letty, it is not like that!"

But the damage had been done. She could see it all clearly now. She was just one in a long line of women that he had seduced, and she would certainly not be the last one. Perhaps it would be Miss Lymington next, perhaps someone else. It did not matter.

"I should have known—"

"Known what?" Edward cut in, taking a step toward her.

Letitia took a deep breath and tried to ignore his heady scent. She could not give in. She had to break cleanly from him, remove his power over her. Otherwise, she would feel this pain for the rest of her life.

"I should have known you were such a rake I could not trust you," Letitia said quietly. "If matters had been reversed, you know what society would have called you? Not a rake, or a cad, which are masculine and delightful things. No, Edward, you would be considered a harlot."

Edward's mouth fell open in genuine surprise, and Letitia felt her cheeks burn to have such a word come from her mouth.

But she could not help it. She had been a fool to think she could change him. Of all people to tame Edward, she was not the one to do it.

"For the first time in my life, I am going to stand up for myself and what I think I am worth," breathed Letitia, trying to keep her voice steady. "And I think I am worth more than this."

"You are," said Edward eagerly.

"When we made love, was the act itself not a promise for something deeper?"

"Letty, my darling, I never promised anything, and we were never engaged."

The words did not make sense.

Letitia swallowed. He did not seem to be teasing her, and there was no playfulness in his tone. Did he believe that they never had an understanding?

She thought back wildly to that night.

"I feel more passionately about you, Lady Letitia Cavendish, than anyone else I have ever met. I have bedded other women. I have not made love to them. I want to make love to you."

Try as she might, Letitia could not remember

any words from that wonderful and now bittersweet night about an engagement.

Letitia stared at Edward in horror. "Do you…do you think I would have let you—let you make love to me if I did not think you were serious in your intentions?"

He swallowed. "I asked to make love to you, and…and you let me. At no point—"

Letitia could not permit this to continue. "Please stop."

Anger bubbled up to the surface again, not at Edward but at herself. She was so furious with herself that she could barely think.

How had she managed to get herself in this position? Was she so foolish to welcome a gentleman into her bed without any sort of assurance he wished to marry her? Had she been so intoxicated with his presence she had completely lost her mind and her maidenhead in the same evening?

"Your carriage, my lady." The footman appeared by her side.

"Let me." Edward stepped forward, hand outstretched to help her into the carriage, but Letitia did not need him.

She did not need anyone anymore. This was what happened when you allowed yourself to care, to feel, to be open and vulnerable with someone else.

She should have stayed a wallflower. If only her cousin Monty had listened all those weeks ago and refused to introduce her to Edward. How many tears would that have prevented?

"I think you have done enough damage to my reputation, Viscount Wynn," she said coldly. "I think it best if we do not see each other again. Thank you."

Her last words were for the footman, who opened the door and helped her swiftly into the carriage.

"But—I want to see you again."

Edward's voice sounded frantic, and Letitia forced her heart to harden. He was not the gentleman she thought. He was not the man who was going to change her life—or perhaps, after all, he was.

But not for the better.

"Well, I do not," she said curtly. "Drive on."

The carriage lurched into motion, and she turned away from the window.

Then, and only then did she give in to the instinct which had sparked when she had heard him speak with Miss Lymington and allowed herself to curl into a ball on the carriage seat and cry.

CHAPTER SIXTEEN

LETITIA DROPPED THE book she'd been half-reading into her lap, rubbing her eyes with one hand. Surely *A New Mathematical and Philosophical Dictionary* could not be this dull for the entirety of its…

She flicked through to the last page and sighed. Three hundred and ninety-four pages. Why had she allowed Mariah to recommend this book?

Because Mariah had nagged and nagged until Letitia had given in and accepted it as her next read.

Was there a bluestocking like Mariah? She had even been talking recently of university education for women, which to Letitia sounded ridiculous.

The weighty tome was heavy in her lap but was nothing compared to the endless weight in her heart.

Edward.

Despite the pain every memory brought her, she could not help herself.

"Anything that I can get you, my lady?"

She had not noticed Bentliff enter the room.

The butler looked anxious. "I do apologize, my lady, I did not mean to startle you."

Letitia smiled. "Please do not worry about it, Bentliff, I was lost in…in my thoughts."

The butler glanced at the book. "Another one of Miss Wynn's gifts, I see."

She nodded. "I am afraid so. You are more than welcome to it when I am finished."

Bentliff grinned and bowed his head. "You are too kind, my lady. And did you have an enjoyable time at the Axwick ball?"

Her smile disappeared. She would have to harden herself to questions like this. Her parents would undoubtedly have similar inquiries, and if she were going to endure supper with them this evening, she would need to find grit within herself.

"I…I shared some kind words with the Duchess of Axwick," she managed to say. "She was most gracious to me."

The butler nodded approvingly. "I have heard many good things about Her Grace. I am glad you experienced a pleasant evening, my lady. Now unless there is anything else, there is a great deal of silver that needs polishing. If you need me, ring the bell."

Letitia leaned back on the sofa. Had she been too foolish? After so many years of guarding her reputation, ensuring she was never left alone with a gentleman, had she opened herself not just to ridicule, but to a broken heart.

In this very room, she had allowed herself to be vulnerable, to lose her innocence with a man that she barely knew, and now was surprised he did not want to marry her.

Of course, he did not! Edward had no heart, no interest in whether she was happy. He had taken what he wanted and disappeared.

Letitia tried not to think about the way he had touched her, about the sensation of his arms around her, the way his chest had been so warm…

It had been exciting when Edward had been courting her, almost thrilling. It happened to other women, that glorious song and dance between a lady and a gentleman.

She had watched from afar and never been a part of it.

But he had been different, and had not just courted her, he had sought her, raced after her—and as soon as he had got what he wanted…

The inevitable happened, and she had been silly not to expect it. His interest had disappeared, and he had moved onto the next conquest.

Right in front of her eyes.

"Then I will have to dedicate a serious amount of time to your study. And I will have to punish you if necessary."

This was not helping. She had intended today to be a time of new beginnings. She had intended to improve her mind.

Instead, she was sitting in the drawing room, rain lashing at the windows in the fading light of the day, feeling miserable.

"Do not be a fool," she whispered to herself. "That is what he wants."

Picking up the book from her lap, she opened it up and attempted to continue.

New principles and new subjects of investigation will not be expected in a work, the professed object of which is to detail the discoveries and improvements of preceding writers.

Letitia sighed and closed the book on her finger. Not a single word was sinking in. All she wanted to do was go to sleep and forget anything had happened. At least when asleep, she could pretend they were still in love.

But he had not been in love with her, had he?

She needed to forget she had fallen in love, forget he had betrayed her, and forget that now, all the rumormongers would be wondering exactly what had happened between them.

Letitia felt heat pour into her cheeks as she thought back to the curious faces watching as she had fought away from Edward—who, in turn, had attracted even more attention by shouting after her.

She could hardly have chosen a more public way to be so evidently connected to him. No one would be under the impression she and Edward—Viscount Wynn, she must now think of him by his proper title—were not intimately connected.

Whatever the gossips of London imagined, it could not be far from the truth.

Letitia closed her eyes in horror at what people must now think of her. She had not been wrong when she had flung those words at Ed—at the viscount the evening before. Her reputation was ruined, and it was only a matter of time before her parents found out.

Her parents were in society as much, if not more than she was. It would not take long for someone with a sympathetic heart to inform her mother about her activities—or someone with a bitter tongue who wanted to bring down the haughty Lord Cavendish a peg or two.

She opened her eyes. She knew what people thought of her parents; she was not immune to gossip herself. But whatever people may think, however stern her father was in public, she knew he was ultimately far more interested in her happiness than many fathers.

But once her father knew—or guessed—what had happened, would he try and make Viscount

Wynn marry her?

A flicker of hope sparked in her heart, but it died quickly. She did not want to marry a man forced into it. She had seen a few marriages start that way, but it was never a recipe for comfort and trust.

No, she wanted more. She wanted to be desired, to be desperately wanted. A gentleman who simply could not live without her.

Like she could not live without him. She could not even think his name without pain.

The door slammed open and hit the wall. Letitia jumped, her book falling to the carpet.

"Miss Mariah Wynn," announced the footman behind the rush of skirts, looking a little disgruntled she had thrown open the door before he had managed to reach it.

"Is that any way to treat a book?" Mariah demanded, staring pointedly at the book on the floor. She was carrying a sopping wet umbrella. "Take this."

The drenched umbrella was thrust into the chest of the footman, who looked in horror at the damp creeping into his suit. Letitia had to force down a smile. There was no one like Mariah for making an entrance, even if she did not intend to.

But today she did not want to see Mariah. Not when her adoptive brother was already so dominant in her thoughts.

"Good afternoon, Mariah," she said weakly.

"Thank you, Larkin, that will be all."

The footman bowed, ready to escape from the whirlwind of her guest, shutting the door behind him as he left.

"Well, are you enjoying it?" Mariah demanded as she threw down her reticule and a parcel of books in wax paper onto the floor as she fell into the armchair nearest the fire.

Letitia blinked. "Enjoying...?"

"The book!" Mariah frowned. "*A New Mathematical and Philosophical Dictionary.*"

"Oh." Letitia looked down at the book and hurriedly picked it up, sitting up on the sofa. "Yes, it is...very enjoyable."

"That is wonderful," she said eagerly. "I thought as soon as I finished it, you would greatly enjoy it. Tell me, which has been your favorite part so far?"

Letitia sighed and tried to keep the look of genuine interest in the world's most boring book on her face. She should have known better than to lie to Mariah, who would undoubtedly want to talk about every single page.

She swallowed. "Well, 'tis the bit...the bit where..."

Mariah sighed, and Letitia's eyes rose from the book to her friend, who looked disappointed. "You have not read it, have you?"

She smiled shyly. "I have managed to get halfway through chapter one, which I personally think is a great achievement, considering the fact that I told you at the beginning, Mariah, that I *did not want to read it.*"

It was unlike her to be so direct, even with Mariah, and she could tell her friend was genuinely hurt by her words.

"I would not have recommended it to you if I did not think you would enjoy it. Why have you not given it another attempt? You may find that if you tried a little more, you would succeed."

Had she not tried enough? Had she not forced herself through shyness for years in company, forced into society, tried not to care when no one ever asked her to dance, tried to attract a gentleman without being too forward, or too wild?

"I have tried," she burst out, the floodgates of her tears suddenly unable to withhold the pressure of her emotions. "I have tried, and I cannot do it!"

Mariah's affronted look disappeared. "Letitia, what on earth is the matter? It is a book, and while it is one I greatly enjoy, it is not a matter of life or death!"

Letitia allowed the tears to fall. She should have cried yesterday when she had returned home.

"It…it is not the book," she managed to choke after a few minutes. "I…I had an argument with your brother last night."

"Adoptive brother," Mariah said automatically. "With Edward? Goodness, I do not know why you even bother talking to him. What on earth did you argue about?"

Letitia fell silent. How could she even begin to explain her interactions with Edward?

She barely understood them herself. There was something about him that made her feel on fire, at times with desire, at other times with anger.

"Do not tell me," said Mariah, rolling her eyes and leaning back in her chair. "Has he roped you into one of his schemes to ruin another young lady's character, is that it?"

Letitia swallowed. It had been a mistake talking with Mariah. She should have pled a headache and retreated upstairs.

"Do not let him bother you, Letitia," Mariah said soothingly. "He always has a hair-brained scheme to attract the attention of one young lady or another, but just ignore him. He always bores of them eventually."

Letitia forced down a sob. "Oh, Mariah."

Her friend offered her a handkerchief. "Let it all out."

It was the permission Letitia needed. She allowed the sorrow and the fury, the pain and the memories of pleasure to rush through her. Tears streamed down her face, and she raised her hands to her eyes as though that would stem the flow, but now there was no stopping until every tear had been shed.

Letitia could not tell how long it was before her sobs subsided, but when she looked up, Mariah was still seated opposite her, now with a far more sympathetic look on her face.

"I-I thought I had an…understanding with….with your brother," said Letitia hesitantly. "Adoptive brother," she corrected. "I went to the Duke of Axwick's ball last night and saw him flirt most outrageously with…with Miss Lymington. I spoke with Edward about it and…"

It was painful to even think about, but to say it aloud was to make it real.

"He told me that he had never cared for me," Letitia managed. "That he did…did not love me."

Mariah sighed heavily, dug around in her reticule for something, and handed something white over to her. "Here, I always carry a spare handkerchief, you never know when you will need one."

She took it gratefully and wiped the wetness from her cheeks. If only she could wipe away the pain so easily.

"Well," sighed Mariah, finally. "I always knew my adoptive brother would be bad news for you, but I did not think you were going to be such an idiot about it all."

"Mariah, you have—you have no idea what you are talking about!"

"Edward may be a fool," Mariah said matter-of-factly, as though explaining how acorns grew into oaks, "but he is a fool with an ego. That man, and I do not call him a gentleman, has spent the last ten years of his life wooing beautiful women—'tis a reflex, he hardly notices he's doing it now."

Mariah had never spoken in this much detail about her adoptive brother, had never shared the circumstances of her adoption by Lord and Lady Wynn before. Where had she come from? Why did she have such a terrible relationship with the only member of her family she had left?

This was not the time to ask those questions.

"Then why did he seduce me?"

Mariah raised an eyebrow. "Did he now?"

"You know what I mean," Letitia said hastily, instantly regretting her moment of honesty. "You know what...what he is like."

"Yes, I do," Mariah said shrewdly. "And this may come as a surprise to you, Letitia, as I think it will, but you are beautiful. No, do not give me all of that guff, you may not like being looked at, but it does not take long to realize you are worth looking at."

Mariah always was so blunt.

"You caught his notice. You were not like all these other women who were clearly out to land him as a husband," said Mariah. "You were yourself, and you attempted to push him away when he first made his overtures. I honestly think he fell in love with you because of that."

It took a few seconds for Mariah's words to sink in.

"You—you think he is in love with me?"

Mariah smiled. "He is mooning about like you, but in his own drawing room. I have just come from there and in this blasted rain, too."

Letitia's mouth fell open. It could not be true. That simply did not make any sense. Edward had told her that he did not love her.

But was that what he said?

"But Letitia…Letty, my darling, we were never engaged."

Mariah was not one to exaggerate, for she always told the absolute truth.

"Do…do you think I should go to him?"

Mariah shrugged. "Whatever you decide is your business, and whatever he decides to do—or not to do—is his own. I cannot be expected to run about town for the two of you. I have already done more than I wished, but he wanted to know you were well, and so here I am."

He wanted to know if she was well—what did that mean?

"Now, do not obsess over every word I speak," Mariah warned. "I know you too well, Letitia. If you want to see him, see him. If you do not, stay here. I am going to stay here while the rain pours. I will read *A New Mathematical and Philosophical Dictionary* if you will not."

Without another word, Mariah pulled the book out of Letitia's hands and opened it to the beginning, pulling her spectacles out of her reticule and placing them on her nose.

There was silence.

Letitia almost laughed aloud; it was so ridiculous. Her mind was so full of thoughts and emotions, none of which she could reconcile.

But she had no reason to distrust Mariah's words. She had been raised with him, after all. There was probably no one who knew Edward better.

"You do not seem particularly concerned about…about it all," Letitia said quietly.

Mariah looked up from her book. "About what?"

Letitia smiled. There was only one Mariah. "For one of my closest friends, you do not seem particularly concerned."

"Oh, I am concerned," Mariah said. "I am concerned about the right for women to vote, work, and attend university. Honestly, Letitia, if you and my dear brother cannot sort this out between you, I do not think you would have much of a shot at a happy marriage, do you?"

She disappeared into her book again, and Letitia smiled. She could not deny Mariah's words, but there was no ignoring the fact that if Edward truly loved her, would it not be him in the armchair opposite her, attempting to fix the confusion between them, not Mariah?

CHAPTER SEVENTEEN

THIS WAS MADNESS. Edward had never hidden from a fight before, never avoided a lady who wished to see him, never fled from a difficult conversation.

Even some he wished in hindsight that he had. Breakfast with Mr. Pickering after being found in his daughter's bedchamber was still a painful memory.

He should be with Letitia, on bended knee, begging her to forgive him.

The mess he had made could not be fixed immediately, but it would be an ache in his soul until he did something about it.

But after a restless night, Edward had risen early and stomped up and down the streets of London.

Purposeless, rudderless, he walked along every street save where he wanted to go—Cavendish Square.

He had to do something and was too much of a coward. Despite the pain in his heart, he could not lower himself and do the one thing certain to fix that pain, talk to Lady Letitia Cavendish, the shy and quiet woman who had utterly possessed his heart since he had first been introduced to her.

No, instead, he was selfish and stupid. When he returned home, a rather surprised Peters had obeyed him and taken a short letter to the Duke of Axwick's residence. The response came within the hour.

Within another hour, the two of them had fled the confines of town and were now enjoying the fresh air of Hyde Park. The grass was smooth, the park empty, and the wind rustled through their hair.

Edward took in a deep breath and tried to hold it in as long as possible, relishing the tightness in his chest. Better a physical pain than an emotional one.

Perhaps if he stayed here long enough, he would forget the troubles now haunting him.

Axwick, riding ahead on a majestic dark brown horse, calmed his cantering steed to a gentle trot.

Edward drew up alongside him. They had ridden in silence up until now. Axwick somehow understood it was important not to talk.

Edward sighed. "I am almost certain you are

guessing why I have asked you to join me on this ride so early."

His voice sounded stilted, as though his throat had been irrevocably damaged from the sobs forced down. His father had always spanked him when he had cried as a child. The habit was hard to break.

"Not at all," Axwick grinned. "No, it is perfectly normal for friends to send letters at six in the morning, demanding that I accompany them on a ride."

Edward knew he was joking, but he still felt a little uncomfortable. "Tad exaggeration, Axwick, surely? I do not believe there was a demand in a single line of that letter I sent you."

"There were but five lines or so of the entire letter," Axwick countered. "And no, I suppose you cannot say precisely that the letter included a demand. But any letter hand-delivered before I have woken is demanding something, even if the writer does not know that himself."

There was too much truth in Axwick's words for Edward to refute them. Instead, he shook his head. "It does not matter. Forget I said anything."

"Come now," said Axwick quietly. "You are family, Wynn, and no matter how distant that connection, as an Axwick, I am required to support you. What's more, as a St. Maur, I choose to, and as Richard, I want to. Something is eating you up. What is it?"

Edward hesitated, before he spoke a single syllable. This was a secret that he had kept to himself successfully—well, except for Mariah.

He had never imagined she could be so…well, so damned understanding. Perhaps after all these years, they could start to build something like a friendship. It would have made his mother—their mother, happy.

But once he opened his mouth and told the story to Axwick, there was no going back.

Edward sighed. "I know these words do not need to be said, but…Axwick, whatever is said on this ride will stay between the two of us, won't it?"

Axwick nodded. "You did not need to ask, but I have a feeling I know why you have. Come out with it, then. What is her name?"

It was not a pleasant feeling, being so transparent—or having a reputation so despicably predictable.

"You know Lady Letitia Cavendish, do you not?" Edward felt strange speaking her full name. "You were there when we were introduced. How well do you know her?"

He glanced at his companion and saw a flicker of concern, followed by something that looked painfully like resignation.

"You do not have to worry yourself," Axwick said heavily. "My wife has given me all the details, or at least all she knows, so you need not concern yourself with bringing me up to speed."

Fury stabbed through Edward's heart like a dagger, and before he could stop himself, he spat out, "Oh, I see—so the ties of family and blood are not enough to prevent gossip? Is my entire acquaintance with Lady Letitia just fodder for society's gossips? I did not think I would ever have to include your wife in that group, Axwick!"

As soon as the words were out of his mouth, Edward knew he had gone too far. To insult a woman, any woman, with such hot words…

Axwick would be within his rights to call him out.

Edward looked down, and when he could bring himself to look up again, Axwick was smiling kindly.

"My dear friend," Axwick said, shaking his head, "please take this advice from someone five years older than you and much more married than you. 'Tis impossible to halt that sort of talk, and I would thank you not to call the duchess a gossip. It was she whom Lady Letitia turned to in her hour of need, and my wife who called her the carriage that transported her home safely after your…disagreement."

Edward bit his lip. If he had been hoping for any sympathy from Axwick, he would be disappointed. He never intended to do harm, but his tongue was able to charm as easily as harm.

"That…that is not what I meant."

The two of them continued riding. Edward could barely marshal his own thoughts, so many crowded for attention. He wanted to pour out all his frustration and confusion, the irritation he had with the world, and the disgust he felt for himself.

Eventually, he burst out, "What was I thinking?"

His words made Axwick laugh. "You know, I have no idea. You are a complete fool, and I do not even know the whole story. What in God's name did you say to that poor woman while she was waiting for my carriage?"

Edward swallowed. "I am not proud of it. I was base and cowardly, and…I reminded her that I had never told her I loved her. Or offered marriage."

Axwick gave a low whistle. "That is despicable, Wynn."

"I know," Edward said wretchedly. "I was foolish, I—"

"And completely untrue," Axwick interrupted. "I mean, you have been mooning over her for weeks now. If it were anyone else, I would say that you should bed her and move on, but as it is Lady Letitia Cavendish…"

His voice trailed away when he caught sight of Edward's face.

"Oh, God's teeth, man, you did not."

Edward felt his hackles rise. "It is not like your own past is unblemished!"

"Yes, but I *married* the woman I fell in love with," Axwick said cuttingly. "Admittedly not without a few interesting tangles of our own. 'Tis a story and a half, and one day I will tell you, but right now, you have your own mess to untangle."

Edward sighed as the two horses stopped. "I was swept up in the moment."

Axwick frowned. "Too caught up in your own ego, you mean."

"I had forgotten how direct you were, Axwick."

His companion snorted. "That is because you have not come to town for two years. 'Tis easy to forget someone's mannerisms when you never see them. Tell me, Wynn, why have you stayed away for so long?"

It was easier to shrug than reply honestly. Edward focused on the neck of his horse, the way he shivered in the early morning air, still warming up after a freezing night.

But Axwick's question led to thoughts he had attempted to bury all Season. The memory of that huge house, rattling about in it, unable to think straight, unable to leave.

His mother's death had come quickly, his father's more slowly. They had been trapped there together, and when they had finally died, Edward became trapped by the memories.

He had never liked the man, and by all accounts, the feelings were mutual. But when he had died, all connection to his mother had gone, too. Mariah was no help; she had a better measure of the man than Edward ever did. She had left years before, and so it was he who was locked in the house that seemed to be his prison.

Edward swallowed. He never wanted to go back to that dark time in his life again. Escaping into society, first Brighton, then Bath, now London, had been the tonic he thought he had been looking for.

Charming women had made him feel alive. Now all he felt was pain. The old numbness would be better than this agony.

"If I could change," he said aloud.

"You would do the same thing," interrupted Axwick with no malice. "I know you."

Edward sighed. "I hardly know myself. I mean, I ask you, what did I think I was doing with Miss Lymington? And I knew Letty— Letitia," he felt his cheeks crimson, "was there. What was I attempting to prove? To whom?"

Axwick shrugged and pulled at his reins, encouraging his horse into a trot back to the park gate. "Old habits die hard. You do not think that I immediately became the perfect husband to Tabitha, do you?"

Glancing at him, Edward saw a hint of shame in his companion's face, which he had not expected.

"No, I had to learn, adapt, and change."

"I have done my changing for other people, Axwick." Edward had not intended his voice to be so harsh, but he did not want the expectation of yet another compromise. He had done that time and time again as a child. He would not do it again. "My father demanded much from me and my sister, and—"

"Sister?"

Edward blinked. "Yes, sister."

Axwick looked genuinely astonished. "I did not know you had a sister."

Edward had to laugh. "You have met her, surely, she is in town most of the year because, she informs me, they have the best libraries. Miss Mariah Wynn, the well-known and, sadly, poorly respected bluestocking?"

He laughed again at the look of surprise on Axwick's face. "You are not the only one to be unaware. She…she left our family when only fifteen. There's another long story and not my own."

He did not speak to purposefully intrigue, and he was grateful Axwick did not wish him to tell the tale.

"When you become someone's husband," Axwick said with a grin, "you have to accept that they will require different things of you. Just as you would expect your wife to adapt for you."

The sun was up now, and people were starting to pass them. Edward frowned. All this talk from Axwick did not make any sense.

"All this changing, adapting—why not find someone with whom you can be yourself?"

Axwick sighed. "That is the great mystery about marriage. You are under no obligation to change but, because of the love you feel for that person, you find yourself changing unconsciously to make them happier. That is what makes you a husband."

The words made sense to Edward, and he shook himself hurriedly. "I am not her husband."

His gaze caught Axwick's, who was looking stern. "No, you are not. But you should be."

CHAPTER EIGHTEEN

"AND THAT," SAID Lord Cavendish with a dark sense of finality, "is that."

Letitia stared into his eyes, and all she could see was decision.

She did not want to let him down, even though he was forcing her to do exactly the opposite of what she wanted.

"I have no wish to go," she began.

"Your wishes are not what matters here," Lord Cavendish snapped, pulling on his greatcoat and ignoring Bentliff's attempts to help. "I am the head of this household, Letitia, and that means decisions rest with me, not you."

"If she truly does not want to go, perhaps it is for the best if she stays behind," Lady Cavendish said while gazing into a looking glass, twirling ringlets around her finger.

Lord Cavendish slammed the front door shut, and the snap echoed in the hallway.

Letitia flinched. She was standing between her parents as the grandfather clock to the left of the door chimed nine o'clock. They were late. Her father hated being late.

"Your pelisse, my lady," the butler spoke quietly, but Letitia pushed away the garment.

"I d-do not wish to go," she said less firmly than she felt. *When was the last time she had defied her parents, and before a servant, too?*

Lady Cavendish looked away from her own reflection and toward her daughter.

The silence continued, and Letitia knew she would break it. Dread bubbled in her stomach; she was not a rebellious child and never had been. But she could not allow this to continue. She was not the pliant child she had once been.

How could she explain this to her parents, who had done nothing but their duty their entire lives?

"I am two and twenty," she started in a quiet voice. "I am not a child, Papa, and I have always obeyed you on the things that truly mattered. But—"

"Everything matters when you are a Cavendish."

Letitia looked into his eyes and forced herself to continue. "But I do not believe I should be forced to attend a ball if I do not wish to go."

It was the most determined statement she had ever made to either of her parents, and she felt reckless, but it had to be said. If she did not say something now, she would still be trotted out as the Cavendish daughter when she was two and forty!

Lord Cavendish did not agree. "Am I to be disrespected in this way, in my own home, by my own child? 'Tis not to be borne!"

His glare was fierce, but Letitia forced her own voice to remain calm. "It is not disrespect, Papa. You know I think most highly of you and Mama."

She risked a glance at her mother, who was watching with concern.

Letitia swallowed. If she wished to be treated as an adult by her parents, this was the best place to start.

"No disrespect is intended at all, Papa, it is merely personal preference," she said quietly. "I attend many balls, card parties, luncheons, and dinners. I am not refusing to attend them all, but I do not see why I should have to attend this one when I most particularly would like to go to bed early this evening."

And cry into my pillow, Letitia thought desperately. *And wonder how it all went so wrong between myself and Edward, when all I wanted to do was love him and be loved by him.*

Viscount Wynn had not visited. He had sent no letter, no message through Mariah or anyone else. If he had wanted to repair the bond between them, he would have done so. And that meant…

"I do not know where this streak of mutiny has come from," Lord Cavendish said. "This is not how we raised you, Letitia, and I thought Lady Harriet—"

"The Duchess of Devonshire," interjected Lady Cavendish quietly.

Lord Cavendish frowned at his wife, but she was not Letitia. Her daughter saw the glare returned, and eventually, her father looked away.

"The Duchess of Devonshire, as she now is," snapped Lord Cavendish, "would be the most destructive influence on you, but no. Perhaps it is that Mariah girl—what's her name, Wine?"

"Wynn," breathed Letitia. It was painful to hear her father utter the surname of the man she loved—or thought she loved. The name she had thought, for a few days, may one day become hers.

Letitia, Viscountess Wynn.

Letitia blinked and forced down the tears. This was not the time to collapse into tears.

"Mama, what do you think?" Letitia turned to her mother for support.

Lady Cavendish shook her head without saying a word. Her gaze returned to her husband.

Letitia swallowed and tried not to feel betrayed. Her mother had always followed her father's lead, but it had never concerned her before. Letitia knew her father always wanted the best for her—the best gowns, the best education, the best possible friendships. It was why they had purchased a home in Cavendish Square all those years ago, to be close to other noble members of the peerage.

And she had been grateful when a child, but she was a child no longer. She did not want her father to organize her diary or choose which balls to attend and which to snub.

"And when you are at Lady Howard's ball," her father continued relentlessly, his voice calm but firm, "you will enjoy yourself, Letitia. There will be plenty of young folk your age about the place, you should not want for partners—and I insist you dance every dance."

"Now, Thomas," Lady Cavendish said quickly. Letitia glanced at her mother. "You cannot expect that of any young lady, no matter who they are. Dance every dance in public! I will not have it. No daughter of mine is going to be considered a slattern for standing up with five or six gentlemen in one evening."

Letitia laughed, and it sounded harsh in the echoing hallway. "Do not worry about that, Mama. Dance every dance? I will be fortunate if a single gentleman asks for my hand!"

"They should offer for your hand," snapped Lord Cavendish, pulling his top hat from his butler's hands and jamming it on his own head. "You are a Cavendish, and the nobility of that name should be sufficient for any gentleman, if he had any sense. You may not have an elegant title, but..."

His voice trailed away, and this was such an unusual occurrence that Letitia looked more closely at her father.

Frustration, fear, and concern were all inter-twined with genuine love. Letitia almost gasped to see the intensity of how much he loved her and feared for her future.

"I will not be around forever," her father said quietly. "I want to know a good man will take care of you. Perhaps—perhaps if I had been the elder son, you would have more suitors."

Stepping forward and pushing aside the butler, who was brushing dust from her father's greatcoat, she wrapped her arms around her papa and embraced him.

She could not remember the last time she had hugged him.

Lord Cavendish seemed to understand as he clumsily returned her embrace.

"Papa, I will go tonight," Letitia whispered in his ear, "and I will do my best to uphold the family honor—our family honor. B-But I cannot promise to dance every dance."

When she pulled away, her father's eyes were glistening.

"That is all I ask," he said gruffly.

Then he did something he had not done for years and kissed her on the cheek.

"Come on, or we shall be late," said Lady Cavendish. Letitia saw her eyes were brighter than normal. "Is the carriage ready, Bentliff?"

"It is, indeed, my lady." The butler bowed as he opened the front door.

"Excellent." Lady Cavendish swept past the servant and looked over her shoulder with a smile at her daughter. "Think, Letitia, how many eligible bachelors will be there! I hear that Lady Howard…"

Letitia rolled her eyes behind her mother's back as she followed her into the carriage. After moping around the house for the last few days, she had expected her mother to notice that there was something wrong.

But no. Lady Cavendish had never been close to her daughter. They were such different people; one, a socialite who had been the talk of the town when she had accepted the dashing Lord Cavendish; the other, a wallflower, who hated any thought of attention.

The last thing her parents would assume, Letitia thought as the three of them rattled down the streets of London in their carriage, *was that their daughter's heart was already broken.*

Who would break it? Who would even consider her as a potential wife? She smiled.

"That's the spirit," her father said gruffly. "You will enjoy yourself when you get there, Letitia, and you may find yourself dancing with more than one young gentleman who pleases you."

And pleases you, Letitia thought.

What if Edward was at Lady Howard's ball?

She had not permitted the thought to cross her mind, but now it had, her heart skipped a beat painfully.

If Edward were there, it would be in search of another lady to seduce. How could she watch him do it again?

"Are you feeling quite well, Letitia?"

She was staring at her daughter with genuine concern, her forehead puckered into a frown.

"I am—I am quite well," Letitia managed, instantly regretting her words. That had been the perfect opportunity to crave indulgence and return home, but before she had a chance to amend her response, the carriage came to a stop.

"We are here." Lord Cavendish smiled. "I do not think we are required to stay late, merely showing our faces for a few hours will be sufficient. Unless you are enjoying yourself, Letitia, in which case we can send the carriage back for you."

She looked through the carriage window up to the house. It was almost as grand as their own. She did not know Lady Howard well and could not predict the guest list.

Would Viscount Wynn be invited? Could he already be inside, dancing with a beautiful woman?

Had he forgotten about her already?

"Thank you, Papa," she managed.

Her father was not listening. He had already descended to the pavement and was now helping Lady Cavendish out of the carriage.

Letitia allowed herself to be helped down and stood shivering on the pavement. Now all she had to do was enter Lady Howard's ball and dance—or not dance, as the case would be.

She had agreed to come against her better judgment, and she did not want to be there—but that was beside the point. This was what Cavendishes did, whatever was best for the family.

"Ah, who is that beautiful young woman?"

Letitia looked around as her mother spoke and saw a familiar face descending from a carriage.

Miss Lymington.

Nausea rose from her stomach, but Letitia forced a smile as she inclined her head. Miss Lymington curtseyed in turn and brushed past her to enter Lady Howard's.

Letitia somehow found her voice. "That is Miss Lymington."

"Miss Lymington?" Lady Cavendish's eyes widened. "My word, she is as beautiful as I heard, and with thirty thousand pounds."

As soon as the words were spoken, she colored and glanced at her husband. Lord Cavendish said nothing, but Letitia saw the clench of his jaw at her poor manners.

"Your lordship." One of Lady Howard's footmen bowed as they entered the house and handed over their invitation. "Your ladyship, my lady."

"You enjoy yourself, Letitia," Lady Cavendish said with a smile, waving at an acquaintance who had already gestured that she should join their group. "Your father and I will inform you when we are leaving, and you can decide whether to return with us or stay a little longer."

"Thank you, Mama."

Her father had already gone, and when she looked back at her mother, she was rapidly conversing with her friend.

Letitia stood completely alone and took a deep breath. *This was going to be like any other ball,* she told herself. *You will feel alone and ignored, completely invisible. Then you will go home. It is not the end of the world.*

The next hour was spent wandering from room to room, but with the added pain of keeping continuously alert for any sign of a black-haired gentleman around every corner. Lady Howard's house was far larger than it had appeared from the street, and as Letitia walked through the rooms, she encountered some packed with people, one with a piano and Miss

Lymington playing beautifully, another with dancing, and her mind played tricks on her.

A gentleman laughed as Edward did. A musician smiled at the end of a piece, and the twist of his mouth was like Edward's when he jested with her.

Letitia was weary, her heart sore—and what was worse, Lady Howard's set was different from her own. There was not a single person here she knew.

Until she was standing, watching the dancing, as she always did, and a gap in the set revealed a lady seated on the other side of the room holding a book.

"Good evening, Mariah," Letitia said quietly after crossing the room.

Mariah did not respond immediately, but pulled a piece of paper from her reticule and used it as a makeshift bookmark, carefully noting the page before closing it and smiling at Letitia.

"I was not expecting to see you here," the bluestocking said, rising to her feet.

Letitia laughed. "A ball full of music, laughter, and dancing? Where else would I be but standing here by the wall?"

Mariah frowned as she tucked her book under her arm. "You seem bent on always speaking ill of yourself. 'Tis a strange habit, and one I wish you would cease."

Letitia sighed as her gaze followed the dancing couples, moving intricately like a loom.

All she wanted to do was dance, just once, with a gentleman who truly wanted to dance with her. Was that too much to ask?

But Letitia knew she was lying to herself. What she wanted was Edward.

"It is time to accept what I am," she said. "I am a wallflower, and that is what I will be until I die. Everyone else knows it, and it is time that I accepted it."

"I accept no such thing."

Letitia froze. It was not Mariah who had spoken, but another voice she recognized.

Standing behind her, looking even more handsome than she had remembered, was Edward.

"You," she breathed.

"Finally," said Mariah briskly. "I thought I would have to wait forever. You took your time, Edward."

Letitia stared in confusion. "Wait—wait forever? What in Heaven's name do you mean?"

Mariah smiled, and Letitia saw that for the first time, was a rather mischievous smile. "Well, what is an adopted sister to do but play bait? I will speak with you later, Letitia—or not, as the case may be. I have a book either way."

Letitia watched Mariah step around the room, her mouth open. *Bait? What did Mariah mean?*

"Mariah volunteered to wait here until you arrived."

Letitia stared at Edward, who was smiling nervously.

Love, untamed and ferocious, rose in her heart, but she could not allow it to overwhelm her. Yes, she loved him, but she would not allow herself to be shamed.

All she wanted to do was fling herself into his arms, but the pain of his last words to her were enough to hold her back.

"But—But I want to see you again."

"Well, I do not."

"I know you have no reason to listen to a word I say," Edward said quickly, as though reading her mind. "All I ask is for you to hear—"

"You are right," Letitia interrupted quietly. "I do not want to listen to anything you say. Excuse me, Viscount Wynn."

It took everything in her to walk away, but Letitia knew she owed it to herself, even if no one else believed she was worth it.

"Letitia, wait!"

A hand on her arm prevented her from taking more than three steps, and she turned to stare at him, and the floodgates broke.

"Get your hands off me," she hissed, sparks flying from her eyes. Edward hastily let go. "Damn you, Edward Wynn, and damn your sister for leading me to you! Why can't you leave me alone, why do you have to torment me?"

Edward was smiling.

"And don't you smirk at me, you—you heart-less man!" Letitia tried to keep her voice low and was grateful for the loud music and cheering as the dancing continued. "You have no idea, do you, no idea what you have done to—I mean…"

Words failed her as she stared at the man who she had utterly loved, given over everything that she was—and had thrown it back in her face.

Edward swallowed. "Letitia, I am so sorry. I am a complete dog for the way I treated you."

The apology was so unexpected that Letitia's thoughts stopped in their tracks. "I beg your pardon?"

It was then she noticed that his hands were twisted together, and his eyes were lined and tired.

"I was foolish, and stupid, and arrogant," he said quietly, his dark brown eyes not leaving hers. "I do not deserve you—you deserve so much better, Letitia, and—"

"At last, something we agree on." Letitia put as much coldness in her voice and could not help but laugh when she saw his stricken face. "Oh, Ed—Viscount Wynn, I do not know what to think when you say such things. You are a gentleman of words, and wordplay is your bread and butter. How can I ever trust you again? Why would I want to?"

He stared endlessly at her, and Letitia felt the same attraction to him, the same pull that made her want to fall into his arms.

But she had spoken the truth. *How could she trust him now that she knew he had used the same tricks on her as every other woman he had encountered?*

"What makes me special?" she whispered, not taking her eyes from his. "Why should I believe this is any different?"

"Because you are the first woman I have ever wanted to change for."

Letitia gaped at him, unable to believe what she was hearing.

"I know myself better now, Letty, and by God, I did not like myself. You made me see who I am, and I realized that if I met myself, I would not like the person I had become."

"I—I do not understand—"

"And that was when I realized the reason why I wanted to be different was the true cure," Edward continued, taking another step toward her. They were mere inches away from each other now. "You, Letty."

"You are just saying that. You are a charmer, Edward Wynn, and you always get what you want."

"And I want you," he said urgently. "God's teeth, Letty, you make me feel—you make me want to be a better man. You *make me* a better man. Before, when I was alone in the world and thought there was nothing better than bedding a woman, I had no idea that this connection even existed. Tell me—tell me you feel it, too."

"I felt it. I feel it," Letitia whispered, unable to look away. "Edward, I love you, but—"

"And I love you." Edward smiled. "I have never said that before, not to anyone, and when I say it now, *I mean it.*"

Letitia looked at him carefully. She desperately wanted to believe him but would not allow herself to be tricked again. She would not allow her desire to be loved to overwhelm her reason.

"What are you thinking?" he breathed.

Letitia swallowed. "You have already broken my heart once, and if you cannot take care of it, I would rather you leave me on the sidelines of life. Like the wallflower I am."

Something dark crossed over Edward's face, and Letitia knew she had gone too far—perhaps lost their one chance of reconciliation.

Edward pulled her into his arms and kissed her, passionately and purposefully, on the lips.

The music stopped. Gasps echoed around the room as countless people saw him accost her with a most disgraceful display of affection.

Letitia did not care. She was barely aware anyone else was in the room with them. This was enough—Edward's arms around her, his lips on hers, his scent overpowering her, and the sweet knowledge that this was it. He was hers, and she was his.

The kiss was over before Letitia realized, and she smiled at him, the one gentleman in the world who had seen her for what she was, not merely a wallflower.

"Everyone is looking," she whispered, still captured in his arms.

Edward grinned. "You will have to get used to it, I'm afraid. You are going to be the center of attention for the rest of your life. You are my world, Letty, and I love you."

Before she could think about what he had said, Edward released her and dropped down onto one knee.

"Edward," she whispered.

"Letitia," he said with a grin, his dark hair wild and dropping over his eyes. He pushed it aside before saying, "Lady Letitia Cavendish. After everything I have put you through, after all the heartache and confusion, will you do me the great honor of making me the happiest man in the world, and become my bride?"

Letitia's mouth fell open, but she did not hesitate for a single second. She knew her own heart, and now she knew his.

Pulling Edward to his feet, Letitia smiled shyly as the eyes of everyone in the room were upon her. "I will."

She offered her mouth to him, and he accepted them gladly, cupping her face as though he never wanted to let her go.

"Now, really!"

"Is that—was that Letitia Cavendish? The wallflower?"

"God, that's a turn up for the books—that's Wynn, the rake!"

The words rushed over her, but Letitia paid them no heed. The only person who mattered was standing before her. She would spend the rest of her life getting to know him even better than she did now.

When they eventually broke apart, Edward grinned. "I love you."

Letitia's eyes caught a pair of faces she knew well, and she smiled as she spoke. "I love you, and I am sorry."

Edward's handsome face fell. "Why?"

"Because," Letitia said as she noticed two figures struggling to make their way across the room, "I think you are about to meet my parents."

Edward glanced behind him and saw Lord and Lady Cavendish pushing past the dancers to get to them. "Good. I have some wonderful things to say about their daughter."

Letitia slipped her hand into his and felt at home for the first time in her life. "Don't talk with them too long. We have a wedding to plan."

EPILOGUE

LETITIA TOOK A deep breath and felt the shiver of panic up her spine. "I cannot do it."

Her hands were shaking. The fear within her had to escape somehow.

"What?" Mariah's voice was vague, as though she had not heard anything.

Letitia sighed and turned to look at her friend, lying on her bed, holding a book above her.

She smiled. There was only one Mariah, and she should not be surprised, after all these years, to see her acting as she always had.

Her shaking fingers tried to shift a troublesome piece of hair from one side of her parting to the other.

"On this day of all days, do you not think you could pay attention to something not printed in a book?"

Letitia did not intend her words to be harsh,

but they were tinged with the fear within her.

"Letitia, is that any way to speak on your wedding day?"

Lady Cavendish was seated by the window and had previously been giving them a running commentary of who was walking along the street and whether she considered their bonnet to be of this season or not.

Now she was glaring at her daughter. "I would have thought you would be grateful to Mariah. 'Twas her, after all, who was the orchestrator of your engagement with Viscount Wynn, and I must say, I am glad the two of you will become sisters."

"I am grateful, too, Mariah," Letitia said softly, a wry smile creeping across her face. "But I do not think we should give her the entirety of the credit for the engagement, Mama. I think the majority of it, surely, must go to myself and Edward."

Lady Cavendish rolled her eyes. "Edward, perhaps, and I do congratulate you, my dear, because he will make a handsome son-in-law. But what did you do?"

Letitia swallowed and turned back to the looking glass. Her mother's thoughts were almost transparent. It was not Letitia who had apologized. It was not Letitia who had proposed. It was not Letitia who would make an honest woman of her.

But, and Letitia held onto this knowledge like a fire in her belly, *she had never needed to apologize.* She had done nothing wrong, and it had been her demand to Edward outside the Axwick ball which had changed everything.

"Do you...do you think I would have let you—let you make love to me if I did not think you were serious in your intentions?"

"Yes, Mama," she said demurely.

Lady Cavendish sniffed, but when she rose from her chair, she did so to embrace her daughter. "I am so proud of you, my darling. You did not descend to any nasty tricks to land a gentleman, and by all accounts, your Edward will make you happy. Now, I am going to inquire with Cook and Bentliff to ensure that all is going to plan. I will see you at the church."

Kissing her daughter's head, Lady Cavendish paused for a moment and gave Letitia a look she did not recognize, something between intense pride and sadness.

A lump rose in Letitia's throat. "I am getting married, Mama. I will still be your daughter, still live in London in the Season. You will see me every day."

Lady Cavendish nodded, but the sadness did not disappear in her eyes. "Yes, I know. But it will not be the same."

With a swish of skirts, she was gone, the door closed gently behind her.

Letitia stood still, the moment she had shared with her mother absorbing all her attention.

"This is a fantastic book, you know, Letitia," came a voice from the bed, "and you would know that if you had bothered to read it."

Letitia smiled and turned to look at Mariah. "It is not *A New Mathematical and Philosophical Dictionary* again, is it?"

Mariah sat up and crossed her legs, grinning. "I honestly believe you would find it a most instructive text."

"Do you think today we could not focus on the books that I should have read, and instead whether or not I am going to go through with this and…and marry your brother?"

"Adoptive brother," came Mariah's automatic response, then her gray eyes sharpened. "Do you mean to say…do you mean you are having second thoughts, cold feet? Am I about to help you escape to the continent?"

Letitia laughed as she stepped across the room and dropped onto the bed. "Whether or not I get married today, I think we can agree that I would never have the bravery to escape to anywhere."

But Mariah was no longer laughing. She reached and took Letitia's hand in hers. "If you do not want to marry him…"

"'Tis not that, exactly." Letitia could barely understand the panic herself. "I am not sure whether I can go into that church with everyone looking at me."

Just the thought of people watching her, judging her, making comments about her gown, her hair, whether or not Edward was a fool to marry her...

Mariah smiled wistfully. "Do you remember Miss Gray?"

Letitia started. "Miss Gray?"

Mariah nodded. "The governess we shared when we were young."

"Only for a summer, if I remember rightly." Letitia tried to think back. She hadn't met Edward that summer; he had been sent away for a reason she had never known. "She was formidable if I remember correctly."

"A true bluestocking," said Mariah proudly, a fondness in her voice that rarely crept in. "She told you off once, do you remember, for not completing your mathematics exercises correctly."

Letitia remembered, and another detail came to mind. "Was that the same day that she chastised you for completing the next chapter early, before we had got to it?"

Mariah giggled, her chestnut hair catching the light and her spectacles sparkling. "Even then, I had far more interest in books than gentlemen. Even then, with just the three of us in that schoolroom, I could see how mortified the attention made you."

Letitia's smile disappeared. The memory was sharp now. She could almost smell the mustiness of the schoolroom. *Oh, how she had burned with shame as Miss Gray had pointed out her mistakes.*

"I have never sought the spotlight," she said quietly. "And today will be focused on me."

It was impossible to prevent the fear and anxiety flowing into her voice. The thought of meeting Edward at the end of the aisle was not enough to still her frantically beating heart.

Mariah smiled wryly. "Does a small part of you think you will go up the aisle with your father, and Edward won't be there?"

Letitia nodded. It pained her to think so negatively about the man soon to become her husband, but he had not exactly given her overwhelming evidence of his reliability.

"I know he cares about me, but he is changing so much for me, leaving behind so many habits," Letitia said quietly. "What if he has woken today and realized I am not worth it? There are so many other young ladies out there, so many other women he has not met. What if one of them…"

Her voice trailed away. She could not bear to think the words hiding in her heart.

Mariah said nothing but rose from the bed, pulling Letitia with her. They stood hands together, Mariah looking fiercely into her eyes.

"Then he is not worth it," she said finally.

"And that will be an end to it. Besides, he would have to be a fool to think he could never change. He has already changed so much—remember how he spoke to your father last night at dinner."

Letitia smiled. She had never expected anyone to take the time to discover her father's quirks, but even Lord Cavendish was not totally immune to Edward's charms. Within the hour, they were happily comparing the texture and flavor of different cigars.

"He never bothered with that before," Mariah said quietly. "I have never seen him dedicate time to ensure he was accepted by anyone, Letitia. He is serious in his intentions towards you. Put those worries from your mind."

Letitia smiled through the tears threatening to fall. Mariah was right. Edward had proven himself over the last few weeks to be a gentleman of honor. Now all she needed to do was overcome her own fears.

"This is a day to enjoy!" Mariah's earnestness was catching. "There we go. Now, when do we need to leave to reach the church in time?"

Letitia dropped her friend's hands and glanced at the clock above her mantlepiece.

"Five minutes ago!"

Letitia grabbed the posy of flowers, waiting in a vase by her looking glass.

"We are late," said Lord Cavendish peevishly as they descended the stairs.

Letitia swallowed. "My apologies, Papa."

"My fault, Lord Cavendish," said Mariah quietly. "But did not Aesop say that slow and steady wins the race? I, myself, follow the edicts of Newton, who believed time to be a construct that—"

"Thank you, Mariah," Letitia interrupted hastily. She knew that look on her father's face. "We are ready now, Papa."

Lord Cavendish's eyes moved from Mariah, a friend he evidently thought most unsuitable for his daughter.

His face softened. "You look beautiful, Letitia. Like your mother."

Warmth spread across Letitia's heart, melting away her fear. Her father rarely complimented her, and she could see in his face he meant every word.

"Now, if we are going to prevent heartache for a particular young gentleman," Lord Cavendish said brusquely, "we should probably think about going. Your mother is already there."

Letitia nodded and took her father's arm.

She barely knew how they reached the church. It felt like only a few minutes before she was standing outside, bells pealing, roses around the door which matched the posy in her hand.

"I cannot believe it," she breathed.

Two months ago, she was a wallflower with whom no one wanted to dance. She was a joke to those around her, the poor Cavendish girl who was so shy, no gentleman ever wanted to stand up with her.

Now she was about to stand up with one of the biggest rakes, and not just stand up in a dance set, but in church to become husband and wife.

Assuming he *was* waiting for her.

"Time to go in, Letitia," said Lord Cavendish quietly.

Within a heartbeat, she was standing before Edward, Viscount Wynn—but she had no memory of passing the numerous faces in the church.

She looked into his dark eyes and smiled as she saw her future. How was it possible she, of all the young ladies in the world, was so fortunate to catch his eye and capture his heart?

What had she done to be so fortunate?

"Who brings this woman to be married to this man?"

Letitia felt her father hesitate, and then he said, "I do."

Edward bowed low as Letitia's hand was passed over to his. Her father was gone, and she was left alone at the altar with the vicar and Edward. She smiled at the man she loved, and he grinned back.

"The vows you are about to take—"

"I thought you would never get here," Edward whispered.

"Neither did I."

The first gentleman to see more in her than she did herself. The first and last gentleman to make love to her.

Her husband.

"—pronounce you man and wife," said the vicar grandly, opening up his arms.

Edward squeezed her hand, and as they stepped out of the church, he pulled her into his arms.

"I have been looking forward to this all day," he growled before kissing her with a desperation mirrored by her own heart.

When they broke apart, there were mutterings and some rather scandalized looks.

"What, kiss me?"

Edward smiled. "No, kiss my wife."

Joy she had never known before rose in Letitia's heart, and ignoring the increasing gasps and one woman's tutting, she pulled Edward toward her and threw her arms around his neck as she kissed him.

"And what was that for?" Edward whispered as the kiss ended.

"Because I can."

She had thought the wedding ceremony would be the most uncomfortable part of the day, but Letitia was wrong. It was not until they returned to Cavendish Square did her mother's enthusiasm became apparent.

"God in his Heaven, half of society is here!" Edward stared at the numerous carriages trundling around the square.

Letitia sighed. "I should have expected it. I am their only child, after all. This is the only wedding celebration they will host."

It was a whirlwind inside. Everyone wanted to wish them well, including plenty of her parents' friends and acquaintances who Letitia had never met.

"Oh, your mother and I were such firm friends when we were your age," said a matronly looking woman who pinched Edward's cheek. "And I am so thrilled for you, Louisa."

"Letitia," Edward growled, but he went unnoticed as another couple moved forward to congratulate them. "And just where do you think you are going?"

Letitia smiled. She had taken a few steps away but turned back to explain with one word. "Mariah."

Her friend was half-hidden behind one of her mother's overly large plants. *A New Mathematical and Philosophical Dictionary* had escaped her reticule, and Mariah was utterly absorbed, oblivious to the bustle of the wedding party.

"Mariah," Letitia said quietly as she approached her. "I had hoped you would enjoy yourself."

Mariah looked up, her spectacles half falling

down her nose. "Enjoy myself? I am enjoying myself. Did you know—"

But she was interrupted by Letitia's giggle. "You know, I never thought I would be the one encouraging someone else to dance!"

Mariah closed the book on her finger. "I know, 'tis a rather strange turn of events, isn't it? But you are happy, that is what matters, even if it is with my brother."

"Adoptive brother," Letitia teased gently. "And one day, now that you are my sister, Mariah, I want to hear more about what happened between the two of you."

A shadow passed over Mariah's face, and she looked down at her closed book before she replied. "Perhaps, one day, but not today. It is not a story for a wedding."

Curiosity piqued, Letitia wanted to ask more but knew better than anyone the sign of someone who wanted to be left alone.

"If you want to stay here and continue reading, of course, you can," she said softly.

Mariah nodded gratefully. "If I am ever going to get a good university education, I need to read—"

"Stop badgering my sister and come here!" Edward interrupted inelegantly, crashing to a halt and grinning. "And you abandoned me with more wedding guests than I know what to do with."

Edward pulled her across the room, she could not help a small pang of concern. Mariah Wynn, the eternal bluestocking. Her devotion to her studies trumped all else.

"And now," said Edward quietly, "that is better."

They had emerged into an empty corridor, the noise of the wedding reception disappearing.

Letitia leaned against the wall and breathed out heavily. "Just the two of us."

A mischievous grin appeared on Edward's face. "Just how I like it."

Before Letitia could say anything, he had covered her body with his and was kissing her more passionately than she could ever remember.

She allowed herself to be overcome by the kiss for a moment, then remembered where she was and pushed him away.

"Edward, we cannot possibly—not here!"

Her husband grinned. "Oh, everyone else is celebrating. What are the chances that someone is going to come along here?"

Letitia bit her lip and looked along the corridor. It was rarely used.

A wild sense of abandon overwhelmed her as the desire to be touched by her husband rose. It was thrilling.

"Hardly ever," she whispered, reaching for his hand—but instead of interlocking her fingers with his, she guided his hand, amazed at her own brazenness, to that special place between her thighs that was throbbing for his touch.

Edward laughed as he nuzzled her neck. "God, Letitia, I promise you—this is the only kind of wallflower you will ever be again."

About Emily E K Murdoch

If you love falling in love, then you've come to the right place.

I am a historian and writer and have a varied career to date: from examining medieval manuscripts to designing museum exhibitions, to working as a researcher for the BBC to working for the National Trust.

My books range from England 1050 to Texas 1848, and I can't wait for you to fall in love with my heroes and heroines!

Follow me on twitter and instagram @emilyekmurdoch, find me on facebook at facebook.com/theemilyekmurdoch, and read my blog at www.emilyekmurdoch.com.